"You can call for the driver whenever you are ready. Or," Khalid added, for he could resist her no more, "you can come back to my hotel room."

"I'd like that," Aubrey said, for it was the truth. She wanted to be with Khalid, even if just for a night. She wanted him to be her first, yet he considered her way more experienced than she was. And if she told him her truth? Aubrey was rather certain that Khalid would politely wish her good-night.

And so she lied by omission and chose not to tell Khalid her innocent truth, and as he moved in to kiss her, his eyes still did not look away. Aubrey could feel the warmth of his mouth even before their lips had met.

Aubrey had truly never known a kiss, but even with nothing to compare it to she knew that his kiss was pure bliss. She could not have fathomed how, with such a gentle touch, her heart might tumble. It was as if he had found the weak spot within, the fracture line that, correctly tapped, might shatter her.

"You understand that you won't be sleeping in the guest room?"

Oh, she did. Her lips ached for his, and Khalid's hands on her hips were necessary for they held hers slightly back and prevented them from melding into his, as they felt inclined to do, and so she answered him honestly. "I do."

"Then come to bed."

Secret Heirs of Billionaires

There are some things money can't buy...

Living life at lightning pace, these magnates are no strangers to stakes at their highest. It seems they've got it all... That is, until they find out that there's an unplanned item to add to their list of accomplishments!

Achieved:

1. Successful business empire.

2. Beautiful women in their bed.

3. *An heir to bear their name?*

Though every billionaire needs to leave his legacy in safe hands, discovering a secret heir shakes up the carefully orchestrated plan in more ways than one!

Uncover their secrets in:

The Baby the Billionaire Demands by Jennie Lucas

Married for His One-Night Heir by Jennifer Hayward

The Secret Kept from the Italian by Kate Hewitt

Demanding His Secret Son by Louise Fuller

The Sheikh's Secret Baby by Sharon Kendrick

The Sicilian's Secret Son by Angela Bissell

Look out for more stories in the Secret Heirs of Billionaires series coming soon!

Carol Marinelli

——

CLAIMED FOR THE
SHEIKH'S SHOCK SON

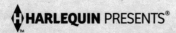

Recycling programs
for this product may
not exist in your area.

ISBN-13: 978-1-335-47825-2

Claimed for the Sheikh's Shock Son

First North American publication 2019

Copyright © 2019 by Carol Marinelli

Printed in U.S.A.

Carol Marinelli recently filled in a form asking for her job title. Thrilled to be able to put down her answer, she put "writer." Then it asked what Carol did for relaxation and she put down the truth—"writing." The third question asked for her hobbies. Well, not wanting to look obsessed, she crossed her fingers and answered "swimming"—but given that the chlorine in the pool does terrible things to her highlights, I'm sure you can guess the real answer!

Books by Carol Marinelli

Harlequin Presents

Secret Heirs of Billionaires

Claiming His Hidden Heir

Billionaires & One-Night Heirs

The Innocent's Secret Baby
Bound by the Sultan's Baby
Sicilian's Baby of Shame

Ruthless Royal Sheikhs

Captive for the Sheikh's Pleasure

The Billionaire's Legacy

Di Sione's Innocent Conquest

The Ruthless Deveraux Brothers

The Innocent's Shock Pregnancy
The Billionaire's Christmas Cinderella

Visit the Author Profile page
at Harlequin.com for more titles.

Dear Alex,
with love, always xxxx

CHAPTER ONE

'WILL YOU BE speaking at the funeral, Your Highness?'

The questions from the paparazzi started even before Sheikh Prince Khalid of Al-Zahan had stepped out of the luxury vehicle.

Jobe Devereux's funeral was tomorrow. The press and television crews were gathered outside the late, great man's Fifth Avenue home, capturing images of visitors arriving to pay their condolences.

Some visitors walked slowly, keen to be photographed and *seen*, others put their heads down and hurried from their cars to the residence.

Others opted to use the trade entrance.

Khalid did neither.

He had flown to New York from Al-Zahan and at the family's request had come directly from the royal jet to Jobe's home. Tomorrow Khalid would be clean-shaven with his thick, black hair freshly cut and he would be wearing a suit. Tonight, though, having come from a retreat in the desert, he was bearded and his tall frame was dressed in dark robes. Khalid was a striking man—tall and slim yet muscular too. Despite his impressive physique he moved in an elegant, unhurried fashion towards the home that he knew well, ignoring the paparazzi's questions. For Khalid, the presence of the press had barely registered and certainly he didn't deign to respond. His mind was elsewhere, for he had lost not just a business partner but someone he both valued and respected.

Yet they persisted.

'Will Chantelle be seated with the family?'

'Might there be some unexpected guests?'

'Your Highness, is it true that the King of Al-Zahan is soon to announce your marriage?'

The last question jarred, not that Khalid showed it. But at home the pressure on him to marry was immense. That it was now being aired here in New York, the place he considered his bolthole, now rendered the pressure inescapable.

The door was opened by the housekeeper and as he stepped inside it was clear that even prior to the funeral, Jobe had pulled in quite a crowd. People were mingling and spilling out from the reception room where groups stood talking. Drinks were being served as if the funeral had already taken place.

Khalid was not here to socialise, though, and was taken straight through to Jobe's study.

'I'll let Ethan know that you're here,' the housekeeper said. 'He's just speaking with the senator.'

'Tell him there is no rush,' Khalid said.

'Is there anything I can get for you?' she checked, 'He shouldn't be long.'

'I'll be fine,' Khalid said, but as the housekeeper headed out the door he called to her. 'Barb,' Khalid said. 'I am sorry for your loss.'

She gave him a watery smile. 'Thank you, Khalid.'

It was a relief to be here in the study and away from the hordes. Khalid could, of course, be polite and make small-talk—his royal status demanded it. He was in no mood to, though.

How odd that one room in a house so far from home could hold so many memories. Jobe's globe had always been a draw for Khalid. It had been an antique when Jobe had purchased it and Khalid would look at all the old countries now gone, while his island country, independent from the mainland, remained.

And it was from this very decanter that Khalid had first tasted alcohol. On that desk that the first tentative sketch of the Royal Al-Zahan Hotel had been drafted.

It was just a year off completion now.

An impossible dream, first born in this study.

Khalid picked up a heavy paperweight and re-called Jobe, for once awkward, tossing it between his hands as a far younger Khalid had opened the study door.

'You wanted to see me, sir?'

'How many times do I have to tell you to call me Jobe? Even my own kids do.'

But Khalid called his own father by his royal title and bowed to him on arriving and leaving, so he struggled to accept the informal greetings in the Devereux household.

'Sit down, son.'

Khalid took a seat when he would have preferred to stay standing, for he was certain he was about to be disciplined. At sixteen he had been in New York City for close to a year and he and Ethan had discovered fake IDs and girls.

Yes, there were plenty of reasons Ethan's father might want to have words with him.

'There's no easy way to say this.' Jobe cleared his throat. 'Khalid, you need to call home.'

'Is something wrong with the twins?' Khalid asked, for he knew his mother was due to give birth any day now.

'No. Your mother gave birth to twins this morning, but there *were* complications. Your mom took a turn for the worse and could not be revived. I'm very sorry to tell you this, Khalid, but your mom is dead.'

It felt as if the air had been sucked out of the study and though Khalid determinedly didn't show it, he felt as if he could not breathe. It simply could not be, for his mother was *so* alive and, unlike his stern father, she smiled and laughed and loved life. Queen Dalila was the very reason that Khalid was here in NYC.

'Call home,' Jobe said. 'Tell your father we can

head straight to the airport and that I will accompany you back to Al-Zahan.'

'No.' Khalid shook his head, for Jobe did not understand that Khalid had to arrive aboard the royal plane. 'But thank you for the kind offer.'

'Khalid.' Jobe spoke with exasperation. 'You are allowed to be upset.'

'With respect, sir, I know what is allowed. I shall call the King now.'

Khalid awaited privacy, but Jobe remained in his seat and then, to Khalid's mind, did the oddest thing. Jobe Devereux put his elbows on the mahogany desk and buried his face in his hands.

Jobe, Khalid realised with both bemusement and strange gratitude, had found telling him hard. It had hurt Jobe to break the news, and he hurt for their mother, and his two-year-old brother, Hussain, and for the twins just born.

Then he heard the voice of the King.

'Alab,' Khalid said, calling him Father.

A mistake.

'I am your King first,' he reminded Khalid. 'You must never forget it, not even for a moment, and especially in dark times.'

'Is it true?' Khalid said. 'Is she dead?'

The King confirmed the grim news, but said there was much consolation that an heir had been spared. 'We celebrate that this morning another heir to the Al-Zahan kingdom was born.'

'So she had a boy and a girl?' Khalid checked.

'Correct.'

'Did she get to see them?' Khalid asked. 'To hold them? Did she know what she had?'

'Khalid, what sort of question is that? I was not with her.'

That he hadn't even found out had Khalid fold then, and an agonised breath shuddered out of him that the King heard.

'There will be no tears,' the King said sharply. 'You are a prince, not a princess. The people need to see strength, not their future King acting like some peasant who weeps and keens.'

As Khalid was being reminded he was royal, and so above emotion and pain, Jobe came around the desk and placed his hand on Khalid's shoulder. Jobe did not know what was being said, for Khalid spoke in Arabic, yet his hand remained, even when the phone call had ended.

'I'm so sorry, son. You'll get through this. Abe and Ethan lost their mom too.'

'They had you, though.' It was the *most* honest admission.

'So do you, Khalid,' Jobe said, for having himself spoken to Khalid's icy father he knew the young man would get no true support at home.

Here in this study Khalid had wept for his mother.

For a short while he had been sixteen and flailing, scared and desperately sad, and Jobe had allowed him to be.

Jobe Devereux had been the only person ever to

see him cry for, even as a child, tears had been for-bidden.

Khalid had been an only child until he'd been a teenager and his brother, Hussain, had been born, lifting from him the full weight of being the only heir. Now there were twins but no mother to love them.

Yes, Khalid had cried.

But by the time the royal plane had arrived the mask had been back on and it had never, to this day, slipped.

'Khalid?'

He realised that he had not heard Ethan come into the study and turned and offered his condolences to his business partner and friend, although they could never have been considered close.

Khalid was not close to anyone.

'Thank you for coming, Khalid.'

'Of course, I was always going to be here for Jobe's funeral.'

'I meant tonight. It's appreciated. How long are you here for?'

'Till the day after tomorrow.'

'You have to leave so soon?'

'I am increasingly needed at home,' Khalid said.

'Well, it was good of you to come.'

'Enough small-talk, Ethan.' Khalid cut straight to the point. 'What's going on?'

'A lot,' Ethan admitted. 'And it *cannot* get out.'

'You know it will go no further.' Khalid was one

of the few who could be trusted with bombshell news. He would never gossip—Khalid was far too remote and royal for that—and so Ethan told him what had been revealed since his father's death.

Jobe Devereux's life had been interesting, to say the least, and had played out in the press for all to see. His sons, Abe and Ethan, had seen it all.

Or had thought that they had.

'There was an account we didn't know about,' Ethan told him.

Khalid listened as Ethan revealed they had found out that Jobe had had a penchant for gambling and showgirls. As it turned out, those long weekends away that Jobe had frequently taken hadn't always been spent at the Hamptons; instead they had been taken in Vegas.

Sin City.

'Are there debts?' Khalid asked, for he *always* dealt first with business.

Ethan shook his head. 'No, he was actually ahead, but this wasn't an occasional thing, Khalid. There were *a lot* of women, oh, and a marriage we didn't know about.'

'A marriage?'

'Between his first wife and my mother, it turns out he was married to a woman named Brandy for all of seventy-two hours.'

'Ancient history,' Khalid dismissed.

'Perhaps, but it's ancient history that might re-surface tomorrow.'

'Jobe's reputation can handle it.' Khalid's words were calm and measured as he poured oil on troubled waters. 'And so can you. Of course, anything that is recent may prove hard on his current partner.' Khalid checked his facts. 'He got back with Chantelle before he died?'

'Not really.' Ethan held out his hand in a wavering motion. 'But they were together on and off for quite a few years.'

'Ethan,' Khalid calmly responded. 'Everyone has a shadow side. And that Jobe kept mistresses, and was married briefly, is hardly going to come as too much of a surprise, surely? Jobe led a colourful life and we all know how much he loved women.'

'Women, yes,' Ethan sighed, and Khalid could see his friend's discomfort and knew he was about to hear the real reason he'd been asked to come by in advance of the funeral. 'For the last four years my father has been sending a considerable monthly sum to an Aubrey Johnson…'

Now Khalid frowned, for this *indeed* came as a surprise. 'Jobe was having an affair with a man?'

And on this dark sombre night Ethan actually laughed. 'No, Khalid. Jobe wasn't gay.'

'But Aubrey is a man's name.'

'Not here it isn't, it's a unisex name. Believe me, Aubrey Johnson is definitely not a man.'

Ethan handed him some photographs.

No, Aubrey was certainly not a man.

She was barely a woman.

Aubrey Johnson had a curtain of blonde hair and china-blue eyes, but her pretty, delicate features were overwhelmed by elaborate stage make-up, with false eyelashes and painted red lips. Her petite, toned figure was shown to effect in a crimson, sequined leotard.

And nothing else.

'How old is she?' Khalid asked, his deep voice hoarse with disappointment.

'Twenty-two,' Ethan said. 'She'll be twenty-three next month.'

Jobe had been seventy-four.

'She's a dancer,' Ethan said.

'I'm assuming we're not talking ballroom…' Khalid started, and then answered his own question as he looked at the next image. From barely a woman to all woman, she wore a tiny, revealing dress and elaborate make-up and his jaw gritted at her provocative pose.

'She's also an aerial trapeze artist, apparently,' Ethan said as Khalid flicked through the photos of Aubrey. 'Though not a very good one,'

'Why do you say she's not any good?' Khalid frowned.

'Well, she's not a big name or anything. Ms Johnson lives in a trailer park and does a routine over the gaming tables. And when she's not performing it would seem she's my father's…' Ethan couldn't finish. 'She was barely eighteen when the payments started.'

What the hell had Jobe been thinking?

Khalid could not stand to think that the man he had so deeply admired would be involved with someone so young. No, he could not accept that from Jobe. 'Could there be another explanation?'

'If there is, we're doing our damnedest to find it.' Ethan shook his head. 'But no.'

'Could she be his daughter?' Khalid persisted, still not wanting to think the worst.

'No.' Again Ethan shook his head. 'My father was a generous man and if he'd known he had a daughter she would not be living in a trailer park. If the money was for a benevolent reason he had trusts and charities set up for that but the payments to Ms Johnson came from the buried account—he didn't want anyone to know.'

'It's better that you do,' Khalid said. '*Before* it gets out.'

'Look, if there's scandal brewing, Abe and I will deal with it, we just don't want anything to hit at the funeral tomorrow. We want our father to have a dignified send-off.'

'Of course.'

'We've made security aware of the names of these women and they are to be kept well back—'

'No, no,' Khalid interrupted. 'You are to let them into the funeral.'

'Absolutely not,' Ethan stated. 'We are *not* turning Jobe's send-off into a Vegas show.'

'Ethan, I thought you invited me here for advice.'

'Yes, but—'

'Do you want a scene outside with the cameras where you have no control?'

'Of course not.'

'Then add these women to the guest list. If they arrive, have security watch them and my detail shall keep an eye out too. You focus on saying farewell to your father. And remember, if any of them do turn up it might just be to pay their respects. No one should be denied that chance.'

'No.' Ethan let out a long breath, but it hitched when Khalid spoke on.

'If they are at the funeral they are to be invited back to the private wake.'

'No way! That really is just for family and close friends.'

'You don't need me to tell you to keep your enemies close, Ethan.'

'And risk his wake being turned into a circus?' Ethan gave a shake of his head, but he knew Khalid well enough to know that he never offered rash advice and so, rather wearily he nodded. 'I'll speak to Abe.'

'This will all be sorted,' Khalid reassured him. 'Your father might have had some secrets, but he was inherently a good man.'

'I know.' Ethan nodded. 'Look, thanks for being here. It would have meant an awful lot to Jobe.'

'Your father meant a lot to me,' Khalid said.

With that out of the way, they went through the

details for the next day. Khalid's royal title had been omitted from the order of service at his own request.

'You're sure about that?' Ethan checked, as Khalid stood to leave.

'Absolutely. That was always the best thing about being here,' Khalid admitted to Ethan. 'I wasn't treated as a prince, or next in line to be King. Here I was just Khalid.' He grew serious then. 'Tomorrow you are to focus on remembering your father. Any problems are now mine to deal with.'

Ethan gave a grateful nod, for he knew that Khalid would take care of things.

As formidable as he was to outsiders, Khalid looked after his own.

'What about you, Khalid?' Ethan asked as he walked him out of the study.

'What about me?' Khalid frowned.

'If everyone has a shadow side, what's yours?'

'You really don't expect me to answer that, do you?' Khalid said, and opened the door.

Of course not.

For no one really knew Khalid.

Here the press described him as a playboy, but that was inaccurate for he did not play.

At anything.

His emotions were always kept strictly in check and he allowed no one close to him, even in bed.

Especially in bed.

For his own reasons he had chosen not to have a harem. He loathed how his mother had suffered when his father had taken himself there. How he had taunted her when another infant had been sired and he could tell her the 'problem' with her failing to provide more heirs was clearly not his.

Those children had no status and were considered unrelated to Khalid, and he did not want those ways to be his own. So he had rejected the harem, but here in New York he dated sophisticated, experienced women who accepted there would be no feigned tenderness.

It was sex.

Khalid's absolute lack of affection was paid for in diamonds, gifts and sometimes plain old hard cash.

Tonight he had plenty with him.

CHAPTER TWO

NEW YORK, THE CITY of Dreams.

And for Aubrey Johnson, New York was also a city of might-have-beens.

How she wished she were here under different circumstances, but instead of arriving in Manhattan to study music, as she had once hoped to, Aubrey was here to say goodbye to a man who had given her a chance.

Only she hadn't taken it.

The day had only just begun and already Aubrey was tired. She was at the very end of an ear infection and the flight from Vegas through the night to JFK hadn't helped matters.

Jobe's funeral was at midday and that it was a private, very high-profile funeral to which she hadn't been invited didn't deter Aubrey. She knew a few tricks and would try to get in, but if not, then she'd pay her last respects from a distance.

It felt important to be here today.

Aubrey headed for the restrooms and there her denim skirt, sandals and loose top were replaced with a black slip dress that she had borrowed from a friend.

It was a little too big for Aubrey's slender frame, but she had a shawl to wear over her shoulders. She pulled on black pantyhose and court shoes. The clothes that she had taken off were neatly folded and packed into her slim black shoulder bag. Aubrey would not be paying for storage.

She took the AirTrain and then the subway and, following the instructions her friend had given her, found herself on a very busy street on a crisp spring day in Manhattan.

Aubrey stood for a moment soaking it all in, her head tipped back as she gazed up in awe at the tall buildings, but she was soon jolted by the sea of people walking determinedly by. Aubrey headed into a large department store and headed up a level to an in-store coffee shop and bought a well-deserved drink.

She had budgeted carefully for today.

For the last few weeks, having seen on the news that Jobe was nearing the end, she had been trying to put a little away whenever she could. It had been hard. Her ear infection had meant her balance was off, and so she'd been unable to do trapeze, and the tips were less when waiting tables. Still, she'd saved enough to buy the cheapest return flights for her and her mom to attend the funeral.

But Stella had refused to come, insisting she wanted to stay home.

Aubrey's mom was a Vegas lifer and loved it. Or she had loved it.

Now she never went further than the porch of their trailer, and that was only after dark.

Aubrey made her coffee last then, when it was done, she popped a mint and an antibiotic pill and took the escalator down to the make-up counter. There she tried lipsticks on the back of her hand until the assistant came over and asked if she could help.

'I hope so,' Aubrey sighed. 'I don't know what I'm looking for really. I don't usually wear make-up...' That wasn't true, Aubrey wore several inches of it each night when she performed, but if her friend was right then the assistant should offer a make-over. Sure enough, she was soon invited to take a seat on a high stool, except Aubrey hesitated.

It felt wrong.

'I wear stage make-up,' she admitted.

'So you're looking for a more natural look?' the assistant asked.

'Yes, but...' Aubrey took a breath. The young woman was around the same age as herself, and no doubt relying on commission and hoping that Aubrey would make some purchases after the make-over. There was no chance of that and Aubrey admitted the truth. 'I actually can't afford to buy anything,'

Their eyes met for a moment, but then the assistant gave her a small smile. 'At least you're honest.' She shrugged. 'Let me give you a make-over anyway. Hopefully we'll pull in a crowd and both come out winning.'

Soon she was sitting on the high stool. 'So where are you off to?' the make-up artist asked, glancing at Aubrey's black attire. 'A funeral?'

'Yes, for a family friend.' Aubrey nodded. 'Though it's going to be very well-heeled. I don't want to stand out.'

'It must be the day for funerals. Today's Jobe Devereux's—' Her voice halted when she felt the heat sear in Aubrey's cheeks. *'That's* where you're headed?'

Jobe was New York City royalty and so, when Aubrey nodded, the make-up assistant knew exactly what her customer was up against. 'Let's get to work, then,' she said. 'I'm Vanda, by the way.'

'Aubrey.'

Vanda plugged in some flat irons and smoothed out Aubrey's wavy blonde hair before taking a very close look at her face. 'You have the most incredible bone structure.'

'You should have seen my mother's,' Aubrey said. 'She had the most amazing cheekbones.'

'Had?'

Aubrey didn't answer. Her mom insisted that her injuries were kept quiet, and even far from Vegas still she didn't reveal how her mother's looks had been ravaged in a fire.

'So…' Vanda asked another question as she worked. 'If you wear stage make-up, what do you do?'

'All sorts,' Aubrey admitted. 'I dance in some shows and do a bit of trapeze…'

'Get out!'

'Nothing too glamorous,' Aubrey was honest. 'Anything and everything really…'

Anything and everything to avoid going into the oldest profession in the world.

It beckoned to Aubrey, of course it did. When the rent was overdue, when the shifts at work dried up…when her mother, disfigured in a fire, *needed* her meds. But Aubrey had found other ways to make ends meet.

Jobe Devereux's money hit her account each and every month.

And each and every month the very generous sum had been spent.

Aubrey had let him think that she was studying music and Jobe, estranged from her mother and a busy man, had never checked.

He'd trusted her, Aubrey guessed, yet instead of education the money had gone on surgery, doctors' bills, medication, rehabilitation, more surgery…

More medication.

Even her mom thought that she was on the game. It was never said outright, of course, but it was Aubrey who took care of the bills and Stella never asked where the money came from.

Aubrey had had serious offers—and some rather glamorous ones too—but she'd declined them all. In truth, she mistrusted men. Her mother had been an escort, that was how Aubrey had come about. Her mom had, for a brief time, been a showgirl, but when parts in the big Vegas shows had got fewer her mom had done what she'd had to to make ends meet.

Until Jobe had come into her mom's life there had been a parade of men through their home, and it had left Aubrey both cynical and scared of sex. Despite the skimpy outfits and provocative moves, she had never been so much as kissed, let alone anything else.

'Don't let history repeat itself,' Jobe had told her.

The simple fact was, Aubrey was too terrified to, even if needs were starting to must—especially now that Jobe was dead and the money would stop.

Still, despite her reluctance, there was an awful feeling of inevitability to it.

That thought had Aubrey's eyes suddenly screw tightly closed, which wasn't ideal when eyeliner was being applied. 'One moment,' she said, and took a deep breath, doing what she could to pull herself together.

'It's okay,' Vanda said. 'We're just about done here, just your lips left to do…'

Aubrey opened her eyes to find that there was quite a crowd now gathered around the counter, all watching the transformation take place.

And it really was a transformation.

Vanda held up a mirror and Aubrey's eyes widened when she saw herself. 'I look…' She swallowed.

'You look amazing.' Vanda smiled.

'No.' Aubrey was struggling to find the right word. The make-up was subtle and neutral and her eyes looked so big and blue. Her blush beige lips looked soft and pretty, and so unlike how they did with the deep crimson she was more used to. 'Sophisticated.'

'You're going to blend right in,' Vanda said, and then glanced down at Aubrey's rather cheap dress, but decided there was nothing that she could do about that. 'I'll give you a sample size of the lipstick so you can top up before the service.'

'You don't have to do that.'

'Have you seen how many customers I now have?' Vanda said. 'I really hope today goes as well as it can for you.'

So did Aubrey.

She might appear streetwise, but she was terrified.

Crowds were gathered and the security was tight, with the street cordoned off, but it did not deter Aubrey. She walked towards the barrier and spoke to a uniformed security guard. 'My driver took me to the wrong drop-off,' she attempted, but was immediately cut off with a question.

'Name?'

'Aubrey,' she mumbled. 'Aubrey Johnson.'

'Wait there.'

There was no chance of getting in, Aubrey knew that. She certainly wouldn't be on the guest list. Still, she was used to slipping into concerts and things and had hoped to find a chink in security's armour, a group to tag onto, or even a less-than-vigilant security guard.

No such luck.

He was talking into his mouthpiece and, knowing that she wouldn't be on the private guest list, Aubrey's eyes scanned the crowd, looking for a vantage point that might give her at least a view of the casket. She wanted to say goodbye, she really did, not just on behalf of her mother but for herself.

'This way, Miss Johnson.'

She turned around at the sound of her name and blinked in surprise as the black velvet rope was pulled back and she realised that she'd been allowed through.

It was a mistake.

Of that she was certain.

Johnson was a common surname after all, but Aubrey took good news when it came.

'Follow that group,' the security guard told her.

Aubrey did so, climbing the stone stairs and then standing in line to sign the book of condolences before heading in. She kept her head down, worried that security might realise their mistake, because she was rather certain that she shouldn't have been allowed in.

And that was how Khalid first saw her.

Alerted that one of the mystery women was here and about to sign the book of condolences, Khalid scanned the line.

His eyes drifted past her twice, but then a gentleman stepped back and he saw her.

From the way she had been painted, from the photos he had seen, Khalid had rather expected a less demure figure.

She was tiny.

A mere wisp.

Her blonde head was bowed down and around her slender shoulders there was a lace shawl that she clutched with one hand.

Khalid made his way over to the line-up. 'Excuse me,' he said to the people who stood behind her, and promptly stepped in. They didn't argue, and not just because it was a funeral. Despite the fact he was today clean-shaven and wearing a black suit, there was still a commanding air to Khalid that had people instinctively defer to him.

In his country they would, of course, have knelt.

Aubrey was far too worked up to notice the movement in the queue behind her.

It was his scent that reached her first.

Khalid always smelled divine—*al-lubān*, or frankincense as it was known here, had been subtly blended with oil of guaiac wood from a *palo santo* tree that had been gifted to the palace. To that there was added a note of bergamot, cardamom and saffron, all blended in the Al-Zahan desert by a mystic, exclusively for Khalid.

It was subtle yet captivating.

So much so that when it reached Aubrey her head rose like a meerkat's and she turned to its source. A man towered over her, so she had to look up from the black tie she first glimpsed. Up to the thick white collar of his shirt and to his throat and strong jaw.

And when Aubrey first met his burning gaze, everything she knew she forgot.

She forgot not to make eye contact.

And she forgot that she generally did not trust men.

In the moment that their eyes met, she simply *forgot*.

Khalid's features remained impassive, yet despite his calm demeanour he instantly felt her allure. From the china blue of her unblinking eyes to lush, full lips, she was captivating. She wore far less make-up than she had in the tasteless photos. Well, a touch too much blusher perhaps, but Aubrey really was exceptionally beautiful; there was no doubting that. Khalid could see how a man could be beguiled.

He refused to be.

'I believe,' Khalid said, 'that it is your turn to sign.'

His voice was rich, deep and accented, and to Aubrey, for a second, his words made no sense, but then she remembered. Oh, yes, the condolence book. She turned from the assault to her senses and picked up a heavy silver pen. Her hand was shaking as she wrote her name.

Aubrey Johnson.

For her address... Well, she left out the trailer park and just put Las Vegas, then she forgot the beautiful stranger behind her and pondered over her message.

What could she say?

*Thank you for making Mom feel like a queen
and for the trips and the fun times...*

Of course she could not put that; his long affair
with her mom had been a faithfully kept secret.

Thank you for believing in me...

Aubrey would have liked to write that, but knew
she could not. Or...?

Sorry I lied.

Jobe had insisted that she take this chance, and
not follow a more familiar, *familial* career path, for
her mother and Aunt Carmel had both made their
living on the game. Would Jobe have forgiven her if
he'd found out that she'd used her scholarship money
for her mom's medical care?

Aubrey would never know now.

And so she wrote a short line and then put down
the pen, and Khalid watched as she moved on before
reading her words.

*Dearest Jobe, thank you for everything. You
were wonderful. Xxx*

The thought of her with Jobe revolted him.
Khalid picked up the pen she had just held and

wrote exactly what he would have before his eyes had held Aubrey's.

Allah yerhamo.

May God have mercy on him.

Those words felt more pertinent now.

'Your Highness.' One of Khalid's security detail was at his side and discreetly told him that another guest on the watch-list had arrived. And then more news must have come into his earpiece, for he added, 'And another.'

CHAPTER THREE

AUBREY WAS GUIDED to a pew and she smiled at a rather overly made-up woman and took a seat beside her, then sat silently looking at the dark oak coffin covered in a huge spray of deep red roses.

Tears sparkled in Aubrey's eyes as she thought of a man who really had been one of a kind and very loved. Clearly, she wasn't the only one who thought so. Aubrey had never seen anything like the turnout for Jobe's funeral. She looked around at the congregation gathered to say farewell to him. They were an eclectic bunch. From *kippahs* to *hijabs*. From military uniforms to medical staff, and alongside New York City's elite were cops and, she was sure, a few mobsters too.

And then her eyes were drawn to the latest arrival. Well, how could they not be? All eyes were drawn to the woman walking in.

She had legs right up to her neck and wore black, although not an awful lot of it, and there was rather a lot of crêpe décolletage on display. Her bottle-blonde hair was backcombed, and around her shoulders she wore a rather tired feather boa that, like its owner, looked as if it might have seen better days.

Aubrey was rather certain she knew her and tried to place her name. Brandy. That was it. Aubrey couldn't think of the rest of her name, but knew that she was a bit of a Vegas legend. She didn't know her directly—Brandy was from before her mom's time and had been a true ex-Vegas showgirl and ran a dance school now.

The congregation seemed to suck in its collective breath, but it didn't seem to bother Brandy. She just swanked her way in on those endless legs as she was directed to the pew behind Aubrey, not remotely concerned by the air of disapproval.

As Aubrey glanced behind she blinked, as she recognised another of the women, and then she looked again at the made-up woman next to her.

Was she perhaps another of Jobe's exes? It dawned on Aubrey that she had been guided to this pew for a reason.

Oh, my, what happened in Vegas wasn't staying there today!

Aubrey actually had to smother a burst of laughter, but as she put her hand up to cover her mouth, she realised she was being watched, and found herself looking into the narrowed eyes of that stunning stranger.

He really was terribly beautiful.

More beautiful than anyone she had ever seen.

He stood in the pews reserved for family. Exquisitely suited, his glossy dark hair was brushed back from his forehead and Aubrey's eyes roamed his face, taking in the details.

Just this morning, when Vanda had complimented her on her bone structure, Aubrey had immediately referenced her mother. For the rest of her life, Aubrey knew, she would now reference him, for the blend of his features was unsurpassed. Caramel-skinned with an aquiline nose, his prominent cheekbones were somehow countered by sensual full lips that were not smiling. If anything, the look he gave her was less than friendly, yet Aubrey found that she could not tear her gaze away.

He did.

As someone spoke to him, he looked abruptly away, yet Aubrey remained entranced and could not stop watching him as the family arrived.

Ethan and Abe were accompanied by their gorgeous wives. Aubrey had kept up to date, via the tabloids, on Jobe's sons.

Aubrey could not though work out the family's relationship with the handsome stranger. And it wasn't to do with his dark skin, more that he did not shake hands with the brothers or kiss their wives, he did not greet them *warmly* and yet they all seemed relieved to see him.

Jobe's partner, Chantelle, seemed to follow his guidance and slipped into the seat he gestured to and then gave him a nod of thanks. She gleamed

with diamonds. Her neat black coat was the perfect
canvas for the most amazing golden blonde hair that
was so completely perfect that, to Aubrey's trained
eye, it just had to be a wig.

Yes, Aubrey knew rather more about Chantelle
than the rest of the Devereux clan.

She had been the reason Jobe had ended things
with her mother.

The service soon started and it really was incredibly moving. The readings were beautiful and the
eulogy, which was delivered by Abe and followed
with a verse from Ethan, had tears welling up in
Aubrey's eyes.

She must not cry here! Aubrey did not want to
draw attention to herself and so she swallowed her
tears down and watched as the stunning stranger
rose.

He was going to speak.

Aubrey glanced down at her order of service.

Thoughts and Poem
Khalid

She turned the page, wondering if his surname
was on the next one, but, no, there was nothing more
to indicate who he was.

Aubrey watched as he walked up to the lectern.
Gosh, he was tall. And his black suit, among hun-
dreds of black suits, stood out—it was just so su-
perbly cut, and sat so well on his broad shoulders.

As he moved the microphone up to accommodate his height she saw that he wore cufflinks, and Aubrey wasn't used to that.

He was just so groomed and polished and, for a short moment, so silent that even a crying baby fell quiet.

Khalid held no notes.

'Jobe first welcomed me into his home one Thanksgiving,' Khalid said. 'I was at school with Ethan, who told me that his father insisted I not spend Thanksgiving alone. We all know the power of Jobe's warm welcome. He was generous and thoughtful in so many ways, and from the smiles I have seen here today, he brought a lot of happiness to many. Yet Jobe would not forgive me if I failed to mention that he was also cutting, ruthless, arrogant...'

The congregation started to laugh as the mild insults continued and his words were both well delivered and accepted.

Aubrey was more than grateful for the chance to watch this intriguing man.

Khalid made the congregation laugh, yet he, himself, did not smile.

He was completely steady, utterly composed. Detached even? Yet his words felt like a necessary caress at the end of an exhausting day, something to lean on as you fell apart.

'Jobe helped many people find their light and shine,' Khalid said, and Aubrey welled up as memories rained down.

Holidays.

Mom, happy and laughing.

The violin that he had bought Aubrey was still her most treasured possession.

Aubrey had been so certain she would not cry that she hadn't even brought a tissue, but when Khalid read a poem in Arabic she crumpled. She had never meant to draw attention to herself. Had just wanted to pay her last respects to Jobe. But the flowers, the people, the memories of better days... Before Chantelle. Before the fire that had ravaged her mom's looks. Before, when she'd had dreams.

Before...

And as Khalid translated the poem into English, his eyes drifted to Aubrey.

Her head was down again but there was a frantic edge to her as she used her shawl to wipe her tears, and Khalid found that he wanted to check in on her. To walk over after his reading and see that she was okay. Ridiculous, of course, and not an impulse he would be acting on, but seeing her sitting so alone and distraught, in that moment it was how he felt. Thankfully, one of the women from the Vegas contingent took from her vast cleavage a handkerchief and, having tapped Aubrey on the shoulder, handed it to her and then rested her hand on Aubrey's shoulder.

As Jobe had once done for him.

Yet his voice did not become husky, neither did it waver as he translated the poem to perfection.

Khalid was, after all, a man of thirty. A man who had, at the age of sixteen, faultlessly delivered a full eulogy at his mother's funeral in front of world leaders. He had been trained for this sort of thing from the cradle and it came as second nature now.

Stepping back from the lectern, he nodded to the casket and retook his seat with the family.

Seamless.

Faultless.

Closed.

Khalid was staying at the same hotel where the wake was being held and arriving there after the service he took the elevator up to his suite.

Soon he would head back down and greet the guests, and keep an eye out, as he had promised Ethan he would, but for now he took a moment alone and gazed out at the view.

It was the end of an era.

Not just Jobe's passing, but his time spent in this amazing city.

It had always galled his father that he'd come here, but his mother had insisted. Khalid used his jet like others might take a cab, yet the time he spent here was already becoming less. He and the Devereux brothers were building a hotel in Al-Zahan, which was consuming. And with Khalid soon to marry and assume more royal duties, there would be fewer trips.

These days he was rarely maudlin but the loss of his mother he felt again as he looked out on New

York City in spring. 'Oh, Khalid,' his mother had said long ago, 'there is nothing better than walking through Central Park, holding hands, kissing in the sun…'

'You held hands and kissed?' He had been fifteen and stunned by his mother's revelations. 'With a man other than my father?'

'Khalid…' She'd laughed. 'I have *never* held hands with your father, neither do we kiss. Oh, *abnay alhabib*…' she implored. 'Oh, beloved son, I have fought for you to walk in the sun and laugh as I did when I was a young princess. One day you will be King but for now, promise me you will have fun.'

Khalid had tried to.

There was another heir, and two more had been on the way.

He could breathe, his mother had told him, before duty called him home for ever. His cold heart had just started to thaw under the hazy New York sun when she had died.

Khalid missed her very much today.

His phone buzzed and for once it wasn't the palace but Ethan, asking where he was. Remembering his duties, Khalid peeled some money from a clip to tip the drivers and bar staff and then headed down to the wake.

In the main, it was a *very* Upper East Side crowd that had been invited back, but to her great surprise Aubrey had found herself being guided into a black car and driven to a hotel, and now she stood in a plush room labelled '*Private Function*'.

Brandy and the others had commandeered the hotel bar and Aubrey was wondering if it might be better to head out there and join them.

Waiters were doing the rounds with trays of drinks and delectable food, but, though hungry, Aubrey declined to accept as her stomach was too knotted up to accept and her hands were too unsteady to be around glass.

Aubrey could feel the daggers being shot in her direction and felt her cheeks burn amidst curious stares. She had done her absolute best not to stand out, but amongst the elite, of course, she did. Her friend's dress was just a little too polyester and a little too big, and the same friend's shoes a touch too long and wide. There were low, polite conversations going on all around but Aubrey stood alone until one portly gentleman came over. He didn't mince his words. 'You knew Jobe how?'

'I'm so sorry,' Aubrey responded. 'I didn't catch your name.'

He blustered for a moment and then went back to his wife and Aubrey again stood alone.

Chantelle worked the room, thanking the guests for their attendance, presumably accepting condolences while sharing small anecdotes, but she gave Aubrey a wide berth.

Aubrey again declined a drink from a passing waiter and was wondering if it might just be simpler to leave. She was already seriously questioning the wisdom of coming back for the wake when a very elegant woman came over and proffered a kind smile before reducing Aubrey with words—'I think you'll find your friends are all at the bar.'

It was the final straw. With her mind made up that she was leaving, Aubrey headed for the doors, but unfortunately, as she did so, the brothers turned from the group they were speaking with and she came face to face with one of the sons that she knew from the tabloids to be Abe.

'Miss Johnson.' He offered a thin smile and a vice-like handshake but even if his stance was polite, his black eyes were unfriendly and the message was clear—*You are not welcome.*

'I'm very sorry for your loss,' Aubrey offered, surprised that he knew her name and realising it hadn't been chance that she had been allowed into the service. Perhaps they knew about Jobe and her mom after all. 'It was a lovely service.'

He didn't respond.

'I was actually just leaving,' Aubrey said.

'Perhaps that would be for the best.'

Ouch.

Khalid now came and stood at her side, like a security guard, Aubrey thought, and it angered her, for they all clearly thought she was either trouble or not good enough to be here.

Aubrey was actually now tempted to accept a drink from the passing waiter just to throw it in Abe's face, to tell him that his father had never looked at her or her mother with such contempt. She was suddenly sick of the Devereuxes and their closed ranks and minds, and tired of being looked at as if she'd brought in dirt on her shoe.

Khalid could feel the tension rip through her, and privately he considered it deserved—Aubrey had been nothing but polite and discreet and had clearly been about to leave.

It was too late for that now, though, for Chantelle had arrived.

Ah, Chantelle.

Khalid inwardly sighed.

She had never quite made it to wife and remained bitter about that fact. Her hair was coiffed to perfection as always, yet her face was flushed from champagne and, if there was such a thing as too many diamonds, Chantelle, to Khalid's mind, was just that.

'I don't believe we've met,' she said to Aubrey. 'I'm Chantelle, Jobe's partner.'

Khalid felt his jaw grit a little. Chantelle had been Jobe's *date* on many an occasion, yes. But the great man himself had kept her at arm's length before his demise.

'I'm Aubrey,' she said, and held out her hand. 'I'm very sorry for your loss.'

Aubrey's hand wasn't accepted.

'The correct thing to do, at an occasion such as this,' Chantelle hissed, 'is to say who you are and your relationship to the deceased.'

'Oh, I'm sorry,' Aubrey said, refusing to let on she was terrified. 'I wasn't aware of that—it's my first funeral.'

And Khalid, who rarely smiled, especially on a day like today, found that he was suppressing one, as Aubrey sidestepped the demand for more information as to who she was.

Yet Chantelle, having spent a week locked out of Devereux discussions and attorneys, having spent a week being less than magnanimously told that while she *could* join the family at the service, the fact was she wasn't one of them.

The Devereuxes were bastards to those not their own.

And Aubrey, alone, stood in the volatile thick of it.

'So where have you travelled from?' Chantelle asked, assuming correctly that Aubrey *wasn't* from the East Side.

'Vegas.'

'Oh.'

Yes—oh.

Just. How. Old. Is. She? Chantelle's eyes screamed as she spoke. 'Do you get to Manhattan much?'

'It's my first time here,' Aubrey answered.

'And you know Jobe, how?'

He had a long affair with my mother, Aubrey was tempted to sweetly reply. *He adored her and treated her like a queen. They used to play strip poker in our trailer. Not while I was there, mind. Jobe was a gentleman like that. He really was. I only found that out the other day when my mom was reminiscing. I was there, though, when he drank cheap whiskey while my mom cooked him spiced chicken wings. They were his favourite, not that you'd know.*

He helped with my homework. You'd twist that and make that sound sleazy, but it never, ever was. He took us to Disney and to see the Hoover Dam and we went in a helicopter over the Grand Canyon. Me! A girl from a trailer park who'd never had a daddy, let alone been on a holiday, flew over the Grand Canyon in a helicopter.

They loved each other and my mom never took a single red cent. Not even when she got so burnt, so broken she couldn't afford her bills, still she didn't let him know. She wanted him to remember her as the beauty she had been and the love they had once had.

But, of course, Aubrey didn't say any of that.

She had nothing left in the tank. Fuelled on no sleep and a single granola bar, suddenly she felt a little sick and also terribly close to tears when Chantelle, her eyes bulging, finally snapped. 'Who exactly are you?'

Aubrey could feel all the eyes on her. She had no idea what to say and was ruing her decision to come. Her heart felt as if it had moved up to her throat and she wanted to turn and run.

Khalid could feel her silent agony as she stood before the inquisition.

While his brief was to protect the Devereux family from Aubrey, his instinct was suddenly to protect her from them. As much as he loved them, Khalid knew their might and, aware of their ruthlessness with outsiders, he stepped in. 'Aubrey is here with me.'

Aubrey blinked as *he* spoke and dared not turn to him; instead she watched as Chantelle turned from angry, to confused, to mollified, right before her eyes.

'Oh…' Chantelle's pursed lips parted in surprise. 'I must apologise. I didn't realise.'

'Why would you, Chantelle?' Khalid responded. 'I never discuss my private life.'

'So, how long have you two been—?' Chantelle persisted, but Khalid would not be interrogated by anyone and interrupting the question he turned to Aubrey. 'Come on.'

Oh, the blessed relief of walking out of the wake with Khalid by her side where it felt no harm could come to her. She liked it that he did not take her hand or snake an arm around her waist, just because the scenario he'd created possibly meant he could, and in the foyer Aubrey turned and faced him, and was suddenly shy. 'Thank you for that.'

'It's no problem.'

'I just didn't know what to say…'

'You don't have to explain your dealings with Jobe to me.'

Dealings? Aubrey frowned at his choice of word, unsure quite what he meant. 'Well, thanks again.' She offered her hand and perhaps that was the wrong thing to do, for he did not accept it, though for a reason Aubrey hadn't thought of—'Isn't that a little formal when we're supposed to be a couple? Chantelle is just over there.'

'Oh, yes.' She nodded and pulled her hand back, and then nerves caught up and generated the most stupid thing Aubrey could possibly say. 'Perhaps I should have kissed you instead?'

'That won't be necessary,' Khalid responded.

She flushed in embarrassment at her stupid words but then he stepped in and saved her there to. 'Aubrey, even were you my date there would be no affection between us and Chantelle would know that.'

'Oh.' She smiled in relief and even made a little joke. 'So, no public displays of affection. Noted.'

Khalid was about to correct her—*no, no affection. Period.*

But that would have led them into dangerous waters indeed, for she might ask him to clarify just what he'd meant by that.

And Khalid would *love* to clarify.

They stood in a busy foyer, yet it felt as if only they two were there. There was warmth in the air between them and there was an awareness too great to share with a stranger on a funeral type of afternoon.

Khalid realised then that he had been wrong earlier about her wearing too much blusher, for colour now spread on her pale cheeks. He understood the effect was because of him. Or, rather, *them.* For though

Khalid did not blush, of course, there *was* heat elsewhere. The effect of Aubrey on him had been unexpected, for she was not to his usual, sophisticated, taste.

And, as they stood there, Aubrey found that she wanted to know the name of his scent, and to know how the silk of his suit felt to touch. And she wished now that he *had* snaked a hand around her waist, just to know brief physical contact with this imposing man. And for Aubrey, those feelings were so unfamiliar that suddenly she had to get away.

He was simply too much.

The whole day had been too much and the antibiotics had made her feel sick. She felt overwhelmed and, not so much dizzy, more that she just had to sit down, so she flicked her eyes from his gaze and thanked him again.

'My pleasure.'

Such a rare pleasure, Aubrey thought as she went and sat on one of the plush lobby chairs and tried to summon the energy for the journey home.

Well, not home—her night would be spent at the airport. Aubrey was just wondering how long she could stretch out sitting here before being moved on when she saw his dark suited legs and even without looking up she just knew it was him.

'Are you okay?' he asked.

'I will be.' She nodded. 'I just needed to sit down.'

'Are you staying locally?'

'No, I'm headed for the airport,' Aubrey said, a

little taken aback when he sat down on one of the plump seats beside her.

'What time is your flight?'

'Nine.' She didn't add that it was at nine a.m. to-morrow but she could see concern in his eyes. 'I'm just a bit wiped.'

'Perhaps because you haven't eaten?'

'I have, there was loads of food…'

'No,' Khalid said, surprising himself that he had noticed, but he had seen her decline the hors d'oeuvres each time the waiters had come around. 'You didn't eat anything.'

'No,' she admitted. 'My stomach was in knots.'

'Would you like me to have something brought to you…?' He was about to raise his hand and sum-mon someone, but she halted him.

'Really, I'm fine, just a little tired—I'm getting over an ear infection and I flew through the night to get here.'

Khalid lived a luxurious life, but did understand that not everyone travelled in the style that he did. She was, he guessed, more than a little tired. He watched as she managed to stand and he glanced at her shoes, which were slightly too large, and then up to her face, which was suddenly slightly too pale.

'Well, it was nice meeting you,' Aubrey said, and all Khalid knew was that he did not want her walk-ing off, weary, hungry and sad.

'Wait,' Khalid said, and of course she swung

around. And now he had to think of a reason for calling her back. 'Aubrey, do you want to go for a lie down?' He saw the flare in her clear blue eyes and immediately realised she had misinterpreted his words. He didn't blame her, for even Khalid was having difficulty qualifying what he had just said.

'Excuse me. What I meant was that my suite will be vacant for a couple of hours.' She gave an owl-like blink of her huge blue eyes that forced Khalid to explain better. 'I have to see the family back to the house, then stay for drinks and, no doubt, dissect who was who at the funeral...'

'Such as me,' Aubrey said, and for a second she thought she saw a flicker of a smile grace his lips, but then decided that she must have imagined it for that glimmer had gone.

'I have already explained to them that you are with me.' Khalid could not quite believe he had offered her the use of his suite. Even his lovers did not get freedom to roam like that. Yet she moved him in unexpected ways. 'You are more than welcome to use my suite for a couple of hours before you go to the airport.'

God, but a lie down sounded nice, Aubrey thought, and then remembered she hadn't been born yesterday. 'I don't think—'

But he interrupted her. 'The choice is yours. I doubt I shall be back till late this evening, so there would be plenty of time for a sleep before you head off.'

'Why would you do that?'

'My role today is to take care of Jobe's friends and I believe you are one of them.'

'But why would you trust me?'

'Trust you?' he checked.

Aubrey saw his frown and wondered if she had used a word he did not comprehend. 'I might trash the room, take off with your things,' she explained further.

But, no, Khalid knew very well what she'd meant. 'Why would you do that, Aubrey?'

He was so measured.

And so very withheld.

Aubrey didn't even know what she meant by withheld, except that was the word that sprang to her mind.

He did not jump to provocation.

It was as if nothing could possibly faze him but, most importantly, he did not faze her. Oh, Khalid was overwhelming to her senses, and more male than any man she had ever met, but there was not so much as a flicker of fear making itself known. And while heading up to a stranger's bed might seem less than wise, it certainly beat lying on the airport floor. As well as that, Aubrey had been born with a radar attached.

It was how she survived.

With Khalid there were no red flags waving and Jobe had clearly thought the world of him.

There was something else, though—this man intrigued her. From the way he had stepped in and saved her from Chantelle's inquisition. The way he had offered her food.

And now rest.

Aubrey didn't trust men.

As a little girl her mom had told her to put a chair against her bedroom door at night and as a not much older girl she had stood on a stool to get ice for her mom's bruises from the freezer.

Khalid, she was aware, brought down her defences, for she *wanted* to trust this man.

'Thank you,' she said, and her voice was a little croaky and the flush was back to her cheeks as she graciously accepted his kind offer. 'But only if you're sure?'

'Of course.' He handed her a card for the suite and told her the floor. 'If you're gone when I get back—' He was interrupted by the shrill call of his name.

'Khalid!'

'Yes, Chantelle.'

And he gave Aubrey the tiniest eye-roll before he turned to the approaching woman; he shared with her his irritation.

It was like being handed the sun.

'We're heading back to the house,' Chantelle said. 'Aubrey, I do hope you'll come…'

Best friends now, Aubrey thought, but Khalid swiftly dealt with the invitation.

'Aubrey shall not be joining us. She has a headache.' He met her eyes and instead of the sun offered her gold. 'Rest now.'

As simply as that, Aubrey escaped.

CHAPTER FOUR

SHE TOOK THE elevator to the designated floor and then found the necessary door, and stepped into heaven.

Through arch windows Central Park beckoned lush and green against a stunning blue sky, but it would have to wait for her inspection as she took in her surroundings.

There were powder-blue velvet sofas arranged around a huge, ornate fireplace, and the ceilings were so high that, not for the first time in this city, Aubrey chose to look up and gaze at the chandelier that caught the late afternoon light. There were ornaments and a decanter filled with liquor as if someone lived here, rather than stayed for a night or two.

Oh, she had heard of suites like this. Aunt Carmel had visited a penthouse suite once and still spoke about it as if it were yesterday. Yet she wasn't here for the same reasons as Aunt Carmel had been, Aubrey thought as she looked around.

Even the powder room was incredible, with gold-plated faucets, which Aubrey turned on for no reason other than the pleasure of washing her hands, then drying them on fluffy white towels.

And Khalid had let her up here?

Things like that just didn't happen in her world.

Aubrey wandered around, peering into his bedroom and seeing the huge king-size bed where Khalid had invited her to rest.

It never dawned on her that there might be a guest room behind one of the many doors.

Aubrey wandered in; yet more luxurious than her surroundings was a hit of the heady scent of him. The suite even had its own private terrace and Aubrey stepped out from the cool silence to the bustle and noise and wanted to wave to the traffic and people below.

She stared right down Fifth Avenue and she knew, from her mom, that Jobe lived on this very street.

Had lived.

Aubrey knew now she'd been right to come today to say goodbye to him properly.

Jobe wasn't the father she'd had never had, but he had been the closest thing to a father she'd known. And when he'd broken things off with her mom, he hadn't simply walked away from her daughter.

'Take this chance,' he had said to Aubrey. 'You've got talent, Aubrey. Don't let history repeat itself…'

It soon would.

The bills were piling up, and Aubrey could only make so much from the trapeze. She was good but not brilliant like some of the girls, and she wasn't skilled at anything else. Had she gone to music college, she might now be carving out a career, but even that felt like an impossible dream, because how could she ever leave her mom?

Aubrey came in from the terrace, closing the French door and breathing in the relative silence as she slipped off her heels. There was a gold watch by the bed and she picked it up and felt its weight. It was a couple of years of wages and tips that she held in her hand, Aubrey guessed.

Probably a whole lot more.

She felt guilty for touching his things and put it down.

Next to where she placed it was a thick wad of cash that caused her throat to tighten. Not just the cash but the diamond money clip that held it.

Aubrey stood in his affluent world, in borrowed clothes, and wished she'd had the nerve to eat the plentiful food at the wake. She could ring for room service, Aubrey guessed, doubting he would even notice or care.

Yet *she* cared.

Aubrey didn't want to abuse his hospitality. And so she took a piece of fruit from a lavish bowl and ate it instead, wondering if he'd mind if she took a shower.

Stepping inside the stunning bathroom, Aubrey's jaw dropped. It was incredible, with gorgeous mosaic floors and walls, a huge double shower and also a bath.

There was a little card beside it, reminding the guest to ring #71 and their bath would be drawn.

That made Aubrey smile. She did not call #71, but instead filled the bath herself, adding scented, fragrant oils to the water. It took ages to fill, but Aubrey had another apple and then, when it still wasn't deep enough, she removed her make-up with the lovely cotton pads and make-up remover all provided by the hotel.

She tried not to touch his things, except...

There was a small silver bottle with Arabic engravings and, curious, Aubrey removed the silver lid and saw beneath that there was a glass stopper. There was a heady waft of his delectable scent, and though she longed to remove the stopper and deeply inhale, she replaced the lid.

Aubrey had her first bath.

Bubbles, oils she just could not resist.

She thought she might never get out, and she was all pink and warm when finally she did and wrapped herself in a thick white robe.

And so tired.

If she could squeeze in a couple of hours' sleep now, it would make a very long night at the airport far more bearable.

Aubrey set her phone and then took time to close the drapes on the stunning view so that not a chink of light came in. The room was in such complete darkness that she had to put out her hands to feel the bed. Not wanting to mess it up for Khalid, she lay atop the coverlet and on her side, but no matter how tired she was it had been too eventful a day to switch off.

She had never expected to get into the service, let alone that they'd know her name. Aubrey's eyes were open as she lay there recalling the animosity from the Devereuxes. Did they know about Jobe and her mom? They couldn't. Surely? Jobe had been adamant that the affair had never got out. It had been what had broken them in the end—Jobe himself had been ashamed of the relationship and had preferred to be seen with the coiffed Chantelle on his arm.

No, Jobe had been utterly determined that that secret must never get out.

They could not know about Jobe and her mom.

But they might know about the money. The knot of anxiety that seemed to live in her chest these days tightened. What if they wanted to know how it had been spent and came after her? Had she duped Jobe? Deep down Aubrey knew the answer was yes, and that knowledge ate at her soul.

Might she be in serious trouble?

It was to that uncomfortable thought that Aubrey fell asleep.

And that was what Khalid walked into.

When he'd returned, Khalid had assumed that she had gone, though he'd knocked on the guest bedroom door and when there was no answer had popped his head in and checked.

Yes, Aubrey Jameson had left and perhaps that

was just as well. He could well see how Jobe might have fallen under her spell, for even a few hours after their meeting she still closed around his mind. Tonight, back at the house, when Ethan had thanked him for stepping in and saving an awkward situation, Khalid had had to bite his tongue on a tart response—he had been saving Aubrey from them.

She brought out something that he did not recognise—for he usually saved his protective side for his people.

He tossed his jacket over a chair and kicked off his shoes and discarded the black socks, then did the same with his tie.

Khalid rarely drank, but on days like today he chose to and poured himself a generous measure. He took off his belt, then removed the cufflinks and undid the buttons on his shirt then yanked it off.

That felt better.

He glanced at his phone and of course word was out he was here, which meant offers of company aplenty.

It was perhaps his last night in New York as a single man, yet he had no desire tonight.

Neither had he last night.

Or rather he had a rarer desire. He thought of the blush spreading across Aubrey's cheeks and how, when he had not so much as touched her, it felt as if he had, and he wished he knew her kiss and the sound she made when she came.

Khalid usually cared little for details like that.

He would hit the shower, and then his phone; he would push all thoughts of tenderness aside. Except the second he pushed on the door to his bedroom suite, before it had swung even halfway open he realised that she was still here.

The room was in darkness and when he stepped in there was the soft presence of another person.

She was deeply asleep.

Khalid knew that for she did not stir and her breathing was gentle and even. His first thought was that he did not want to startle her so he turned on a side light.

Aubrey was curled up on his bed, rather than in it, and wearing a robe.

She looked incredibly peaceful and he wished that he felt the same. Today had been harder, far harder than he had either anticipated or allowed to show.

'Aubrey,' he said gently, and got no response. 'Aubrey,' he said again, and she opened her eyes. 'I thought your flight was at nine.'

Aubrey didn't startle.

It was almost a relief to hear him call her name, for it was as if she'd been chasing him in her dream, but when she opened her eyes it took a second to orientate to her surroundings. The bed felt like a cloud beneath her and there was Khalid, his torso naked, standing above her.

She knew straight away she wasn't dreaming and she also knew nothing untoward had taken place. In fact, bizarrely, for an odd second, Aubrey wished she were waking up *having* been made love to by him, but then she hauled herself from that thought. 'I must have slept through my alarm.'

'Have you missed your flight?' Khalid asked.

'No.' She shook her head and sat up as he turned on another side light. 'I had a bath. I hope you don't mind.'

'Of course not. Did you have something to eat?'

'Some fruit. Thank you. How was it back at the house?'

Khalid went to answer, to tell her how fraught it had been. How Chantelle had seemed determined not to leave. Yet he did not discuss his own private life, let alone the lives of others.

He wanted to though.

Khalid wanted to sit and talk with her, to tell her how his day had really been, but instead he offered a more generic response. 'I think the day went as well as could be expected.'

His words were delivered in a rich accent and his English was excellent, yet she felt as if there was something a little lost in translation, or rather withheld.

There was that word again… *Withheld.*

Possibly, she decided, if they were speaking in his native tongue there would be more elaboration.

What she could not know was that this was more open than Khalid usually was.

'He left me this.' Khalid handed her the paper-weight that Ethan had given him tonight.

'It's gorgeous,' Aubrey said. 'What is it?'

'A paperweight,' Khalid said as he handed her the stone.

'I meant, what is it made of?'

'I don't know,' Khalid said, then asked her a question. 'Aubrey, why didn't you get into bed?'

'Because I didn't want to mess it up for you to-night.'

'Oh.' Khalid nodded. 'That makes sense, except there is a guest room. You could have had covers in there.'

'There's a guest room!' She was mortified and sat bolt upright. 'I had no idea. I've never been some-where like this before. I did everything to try and leave it as I found it...'

'It's fine.' Khalid smiled.

He *smiled*. It was the first time she had seen him do that and it was just so unexpected, and so nice, but Aubrey had to look away.

He was naked from the waist up and he was com-pletely divine. The light did not allow colour but she could see the flat lines of his stomach and that his long arms were muscular. She lay back on the pil-lows, holding the paperweight up so that it caught the glow from the side light and Khalid explained why he had it.

'He was going to give it to me as a wedding pres-ent, but then, in Jobe's words, damn time ran out.'

'Are you getting married?' Aubrey asked, trying to fight a curious disappointment, for it was surely irrelevant to her.

He nodded. 'Though my bride has not been chosen yet.'

'Well, that's good.'

'Good?'

'You don't have to explain me if she calls.'

He didn't smile at her little joke.

Khalid didn't even know that it was one. He would *never* be asked to explain. 'When *is* your flight?'

'At nine in the morning.'

'And where are you staying?'

'I'm not. I'll just hang out at the airport,' Aubrey admitted.

He looked at her for a moment. Khalid did not take in strays and would not be offering her use of the guest room tonight. Yet he found out that where Aubrey was concerned it was easy to be kind. 'Do you want to go for dinner before you head off?'

'Dinner?'

'Well, I need to eat, and I guess so do you. It would seem that you have a few hours to kill.'

'Oh.' Aubrey didn't know what to say to his offer, but he amended it before she had a chance to reply.

'I apologise,' Khalid said. 'It would give me great pleasure if you would join me for dinner, Aubrey.'

She had been about to decline, but this uptight man had her smiling instead.

'I'd love to,' Aubrey said as her heart skipped

off to pick roses, but she hauled it back to the confines of her chest. It wasn't a date. It wasn't a date, she told it.

It was Khalid being incredibly nice.

'My driver will take you to the airport afterwards so bring your things. Now, if you will excuse me, I have to make a phone call before we head off.'

She put down the paperweight, climbed off the bed and set about retrieving her shoes, dress and things and then thanked him again for letting her rest here. 'It really was nice of you. I felt utterly drained.'

'Funerals tend to do that to you.'

'Really? I've never been to one until today.'

'Then you are…' He'd been about to say she was lucky never to have lost someone close to her till now, but then he looked at her scrabbling to find her things, and something halted him, for *lucky* did not seem the right word for the situation. 'You did well,' he said instead.

'Did I?' she checked as she bent to retrieve her shoes. 'I'm worried I made a bit of a fool of myself when I cried.'

'No.'

It sounded as if he had thought about it, as if his answer came with thought. So few people could reassure with just one word, yet he did.

'Get ready,' he told her, and when the door closed on her he dragged a breath in.

She was the enemy.

Not his enemy, of course, but she was capable of causing trouble for the Devereuxes, yet he was taking her to dinner? Khalid had promised to keep an eye on her, but even he knew that it shouldn't extend to this.

And he was not thinking now about dinner.

CHAPTER FIVE

AUBREY STILL HAD no clue where the guest room was and so she took her clothes and things into the powder room to change for her first ever date, which wasn't a date.

She had to keep reminding herself of that as she got ready to be wined and dined!

The dress looked a smidge better without the black shawl and stockings, then she ran a comb through her hair. Aubrey really didn't have much to work with but then she found the lipstick sample that Vanda had given her, as well as some mascara. She darkened her lashes and pinked her lips and decided it wasn't a problem that she didn't have any perfume—after all, scent-wise she could never compete with Khalid.

As Aubrey stepped into the lounge, she could hear Khalid's voice coming from the bedroom as he made his phone call. He spoke in Arabic so she didn't have a clue what was being said, she just liked the deep of his voice.

Her bag was over her shoulder and, deciding she might look a bit eager, she placed it by an occasional chair but did not sit down; instead she stood by a window, watching the New York world go by. Khalid came out and retrieved his discarded clothes and started to dress, still talking on his phone.

He poured her a drink, and she smiled and took it. Then he sat on the chair, his phone tucked between his ear and shoulder as he put on his socks and shoes.

Aubrey got back to looking out of the window, trying to be polite and give him space for his call.

But Khalid did not need space.

It was impossible to put on cufflinks with one hand, and, keen to get to dinner and more than used to being assisted, he went over to Aubrey and when she turned, he held out his upturned arm.

Aubrey had no idea what he meant, until she looked at his outstretched hand and saw the cufflinks.

Still he spoke in Arabic and she looked up with confused eyes.

'Could you?' Khalid broke his conversation and spoke briefly in English.

'Sure.'

Aubrey took a heavy cufflink from his palm and what neither was quite ready for was their first contact.

Her fingers in his palm were so light that it felt as if a bird had briefly landed there and Khalid found that he was not listening to his assistant, Laisha, give her long summary of all that had taken place while he'd been away.

Instead he was looking at Aubrey.

Her hair fell in a pale curtain as she fiddled with the cuffs of his shirt. Her hands were cool and her touch light. She was perfection to him right now. But, no, she was a chameleon, Khalid reminded himself.

Yet she entranced him.

Aubrey had no idea what she was doing with his cufflinks and it was very hard to concentrate when he was so close, but finally she got one of them in.

'The other way,' he said, and she stilled at the depth of his voice when it switched to English.

'Oh.' She removed the cufflink and the cuff of his shirt fell apart again and so too did her nerves. His hands were long-fingered and the fine, dark hairs of his arms made Aubrey's insides shiver. She tried to tell herself it was just a hand, just a wrist as she slid in the gold cufflink the other way, yet he affected her so much. And still she did not know what to do.

Khalid watched her.

Laisha was asking for his response to a statement, but he could not answer, for he was captivated by Aubrey.

He wanted her to rest that mouth in his palm, he wanted the softness of her kiss and not to mind that she had been with Jobe. He wanted her touch and to indulge himself in her skin, yet he stood silent and watched her small smile of triumph when the cufflink was in.

Now the other.

He was about to switch hands with his phone so that she could tend to the other, but he changed his mind and concluded the call with Laisha and inserted the second cufflink himself.

'Come on,' he said, deciding that dinner and his driver taking her to the airport was the far more sensible option. His duty today was to the Devereuxes and the murky complications he did not need. And so, when he opened the door to the penthouse suite and Aubrey headed out, Khalid gave her no excuse to return. 'Aubrey,' he said, assuming it was one of her many tricks. 'Don't forget your bag.'

They took the elevator down and she could smell his incredible cologne and the soapiness of him and she felt self-conscious by his side, but nicely so.

'Okay?' he checked, just before the elevator hit the ground floor.

She nodded, and gave a smile, a slightly uncertain one.

'Good,' he said, 'let's eat.'

It was a beautiful restaurant with a pianist playing. There were a lot of patrons, some still in funeral attire, and that flutter of nerves turned into a surge as they entered, but Khalid ensured that things went smoothly.

He dealt with the greeter and then walked ahead to their table, heads turning as they passed, but really she only had eyes for Khalid's broad shoulders as they were guided to a candlelit corner table that was beautifully dressed with gleaming silverware and a small vase spilling over with ivory peonies. The window looked out to a night-time view of Central Park that, had she not been sitting opposite Khalid, would have been to die for.

Yet she sat opposite Khalid. So elegant, so poised that Aubrey felt like a lady for the first time in her life.

Well, not quite. She was so hungry that she wanted to fall on the bread roll like a savage and tear it apart with her teeth, but she resisted and instead she sat there as the waiter went through the menu and Khalid ordered drinks.

'Champagne?' he enquired, but Aubrey shook her head.

'What was the drink upstairs?' she asked, for though she'd had only had the tiniest sip she could still taste it on her lips.

'Cognac.'

'I'd like that, please.'

'Sounds good,' Khalid said, not caring if it was more an end-of-dinner drink. He turned to waiter. 'I'll have the same. And could we have more bread?'

That he was starving too made her smile and he noticed. 'Why are you smiling?' Khalid asked.

'I don't know.'

He took his roll and sliced it open and then smeared half with golden butter as Aubrey did the same.

'I haven't eaten all day,' Khalid said.

'At all?'

'No, and neither did Ethan or Abe. I said to them before I left that those who organise the feast never get a chance to indulge.'

'Is that an Arabic saying?'

'No.' Khalid smiled. His second for her. 'It's a fact.'

Now she buttered the second half of her roll and he watched her lovely pale hands tremble as they held the silver knife, just as they had with the silver pen.

The strappy dress revealed slender arms and clavicles and even her sternal notch, yet despite her delicacy there was nothing feeble about her.

Aubrey was strong.

And Khalid admired strength.

Yet there was an air of vulnerability too and it saddened Khalid that she might have been taken advantage of by Jobe.

When Aubrey looked up he was no longer smiling and there was a pensive look on his face.

'Did you have breakfast?' she asked, carrying on the conversation, just so intrigued by him she wanted to glean what she could. *Whatever* she could. Did he eat down here in the morning? Was he served breakfast in bed, or at the gleaming table in his suite? He fascinated her so much.

'No,' Khalid said. 'Well, breakfast was served but I was…' He shook his head for he had not examined his thoughts this morning.

'Too sad?'

Khalid never admitted weakness, not even to

himself, but she assumed so rightly that it gave him pause.

'Yes,' he admitted.

'And me,' Aubrey said, then looked down at the menu, trying to work out what to have, except there were no prices.

The pasta, she knew, would be the cheapest, or perhaps she could have a risotto. There was no hope of splitting the bill and she did not want to take advantage. And as Aubrey tried to work out what might be cheapest, Khalid spoke.

'So, how did you...?' He hesitated, not really wanting the answer, but the natural question *was* about Jobe. 'How long were you and Jobe...?' Khalid could not finish, his skin crawling at the very thought.

Hearing this confident man waver, confused Aubrey for a second.

And the next second, as realisation hit, his slight discomfort both shamed and devastated her.

Very deliberately she didn't look up from the menu. She just bit down on her bottom lip as she realised Khalid assumed that she and Jobe had been an item.

She recalled again the word he had used when speaking about her and Jobe. Not relationship, but *dealings*.

Khalid, Aubrey now realised, thought that she was a prostitute.

He wasn't the first to think so and no doubt he

wouldn't be the last. Hell, even her own mother assumed that she was one. But that he did hurt her.

All that had been good about tonight felt as if it had been rearranged into a more sordid interpretation. She looked up, though not at Khalid; instead, her eyes swept the restaurant. She could see the glances in their direction and the attentive waiters, and wondered if everyone assumed the same.

Khalid changed the subject then, not that Aubrey even heard what he said, such was the roaring in her ears. 'Excuse me?'

'I said that the music was pleasant.'

'Y-yes,' Aubrey stammered, but conversation was impossible now. 'I might just use the restroom,' Aubrey said, trying to keep the tremble out of her voice then standing and retrieving her purse.

'Of course. Have you chosen what you want to eat?'

'Er…' While desperate to retreat, to get out on the street and first breathe and then run, instead she picked up the menu and experienced a curl of anger entwined with her shame as she scanned it. She had no intention of coming back, and hopefully by the time her meal arrived he would have more than worked that out, but first she would choose something. 'Lobster Thermidor,' Aubrey said, hoping that was as expensive as it sounded and that it might in some way pay for her hurt.

But Khalid didn't even blink at her choice.

It felt as if all eyes were on her as she left the restaurant. Her heart was hammering in her chest and she was perilously close to breaking down but as she stepped out of the restaurant and into the foyer there was Brandy and the other women heading towards the bar. Aubrey didn't want to be seen by anyone right now so, instead of walking out of the hotel, she fled to the restroom instead.

It was gorgeous, of course. More like a luxurious dressing room with huge mirrors and deep crimson vanity chairs, and Audrey slumped into one and buried her burning face in her hands, going over and over the day.

It was not an oversight or accident that she had been let into the funeral. The Devereuxes must have known about the monthly payments into her accounts and had assumed the worst.

And Khalid did too.

Was he expecting more from tonight? Was she to earn her cognac and lobster? But, no, Aubrey thought, her heart slowing down, whatever Khalid thought of her he had been nothing but nice.

She said it over and over until her breathing slowed down.

Even if he thought she was on the game, throughout the day and this night Khalid had been nothing but nice. He had invited her to dinner, and had said that afterwards his driver was taking her to the airport.

She was forearmed now, because if that deal suddenly changed, she could slap him then.

There was no need to walk out right now.

For, so far, he had been nothing but nice.

'Okay?' Khalid checked as Aubrey took her seat, for she was as pale as the tablecloth and did not meet his eyes.

'I'm fine,' Aubrey said, but though she had returned her guard was now up.

'I ordered,' Khalid said.

'Thanks.' Their drinks had arrived and she took a sip of it, feeling the burn as it went down. 'What did you have?' Aubrey asked, trying to keep the conversation light.

'Pasta primavera,' Khalid said. 'It was the first meal I had when I first came to New York.'

And it may well be his last.

'I had no idea what to eat when I came here,' Khalid elaborated, which was rare in itself, for he did not usually bother with sentimentality, but it was choking him tonight. 'My mother had said to ask for that if I was unsure, and so I did.'

'You studied here?'

'That's right—the last two years of school then to college, where I studied structural engineering. Where I live, the infrastructure is ancient, though not as bad as on the mainland. Still, there is a lot of new development now taking place.'

'Where do you live?' Aubrey asked.

'Al-Zahan,' Khalid said. 'An island country in the Middle East.'

'I've heard of it.' Aubrey startled with recognition of the name. 'One of the hospitality managers I know is hoping to get a position there when the new hotel opens. And then some performers I work with mentioned heading there too, then it was mentioned on the news…' She gave a shake of her head. 'I'd never heard of it until a few weeks ago but now it's everywhere.'

'That happens.' Khalid smiled, for he understood what she meant. 'Take the pasta primavera I have ordered—I had never heard of it, and it sounded exotic.'

'Exotic?'

'To me, yes. And on my first taste I was hooked. But then, on every menu there it was, every time there was an advert or a recipe, and I thought, How did I not know it existed…?'

She forgot how angry she was for a second and laughed, but then the hurt filtered back as Aubrey worked out just why she kept hearing Al-Zahan mentioned. 'It's a Devereux hotel, isn't it?'

'Yes. The hotel is a joint venture between us—it's not due to open until next year,' Khalid explained, and told her about the plans for the hotel, though the fact he was a prince he kept out of it. 'It's a huge project—more than a hotel—really, there will be extravagant shows and entertainment. There is even to be a maternity suite on the hundredth floor.'

'Get out!' Aubrey smiled, and despite doing her best to hold back she still warmed to him.

'No, really,' Khalid said, but he broke off as their meals were served. For Aubrey there was a slight rush of guilt as she looked at her plate and saw the very expensive meal she had so tersely demanded. A whole lobster sat in its shell with a still bubbling sauce beckoning. The conversation remained paused as Aubrey took her first taste.

It was rich and creamy and the lobster simply melted on her tongue. Aubrey couldn't remember ever tasting something so divine.

Or being in the company of someone who was the same.

He asked about her family, and she said there was just her and her mom.

'No brothers or sisters?' Khalid checked.

She shook her head, noticing that he didn't broach what she did for work. 'What about you?'

'I have two brothers and one sister; they are all at school here.'

'Are you close to them?'

'Not really, they are much younger.' And with much less expected of them. 'I am meeting them tomorrow for high tea.'

'Oh!' Aubrey said. 'That sounds very formal.'

'Because I am formal,' Khalid said, and usually that was all he would say, and the subject would be closed, yet he looked at her eyes, so clear and blue, and the softness of her smile as she waited for him to say more. He added little, but it felt like very much. 'I am formal, so that they do not have to be.'

'Well,' Aubrey responded, 'I like you formal.' She did, she just did. Whatever his assumptions about her, she felt safe with this formal man who wore cufflinks to dinner and did not so much as touch her elbow when they walked. She liked how safe he made her feel. Safe enough to go to his hotel room. Safe. As if nothing and no one could harm her when he was near.

And, as they still stared at each other, she wondered how it would feel to be held by him. And what she might do if he reached out for her hand.

Her heart was thumping in her chest and she could feel heat spread on her neck. She looked at his closed mouth and, aware of her own now, wondered how it would feel on hers.

She tore her eyes away and looked down at her nearly empty plate and she felt shaken and a bit confused because she had been so angry with him before. Yet anger felt a whole lot like want, Aubrey now knew, for she was hot and bothered, only nicely so. She did not know what to do with feelings so new and confusing so she finished what was left on her plate.

'Th-this was b-beautiful,' she stammered. 'Thank you.'

He looked after her there too, for her silverware was slung on the sides of her plate. And though he could eat more if he chose to, Khalid subtly taught her what to do. 'I have had enough too.'

He put down his knife and fork close together.

She looked at her own rather messy plate and arranged her silverware to match his.

'I'm glad you enjoyed it,' Khalid said.

She had.

And not just the food and sumptuous surroundings. Now the anger had dimmed, she realised she had simply enjoyed his company.

He did not flirt, in fact he made no effort to impress.

Khalid simply did.

It was that he made an effort for her. He had suggested a soft drink when he saw that she was struggling with the cognac. Little things. The nicest things. And when their closed silverware had the waiter remove their plates, he must have seen the slight disappointment on her face when he declined the dessert menu.

'Go ahead, though,' Khalid offered.

'No, honestly, I'm full.' Aubrey said, to be polite, but though she *was* full, she had also secretly wanted dessert, she just didn't want to eat one without him.

'Perhaps I will have one after all.' Khalid said, and called the waiter to retrieve the dessert menu.

She brought out the nice in Khalid, so much so that he ate halva ice cream, which he didn't really want, while Aubrey sank her spoon into a pillow of dark chocolate soufflé.

And he fought himself—fought not to take her hand or to accept a taste of her soufflé when she offered because Khalid did not indulge in such things.

Not even for one night.

'Is it nice?' Aubrey asked of his dessert.

'Very.' Khalid nodded.

Aubrey wished that he would ask for a taste, and not just so that she could then try his dessert. She wanted that small intimacy with Khalid.

For the first time in her life, Aubrey wanted intimacy with another person.

'Mine tastes like heaven,' she said.

'Good.'

'What's halva?'

'It is a confectionery.'

'And what does it taste like?'

'Would you like me to order you some so that you can try?' Khalid offered, deliberately misreading her cue.

She inwardly sagged in disappointment and tried not to show it in her face. 'No.'

Khalid looked at her chocolate-coated lips and it would seem there was something more he now knew about Aubrey—she liked her desserts.

'No, thank you,' she added. 'Because it would be a terrible waste when I only want to know what it tastes like.'

He met her pleading eyes. 'Then you must order it some time.'

Aubrey watched as he scraped the last spoonful of ice cream from his bowl and she wanted to squirm in her seat because high between her legs she ached as she willed that spoon to be offered to her, but it wasn't.

Instead, Khalid did something better. He swallowed down the precious last drop of ice cream and instead of a taste of his dessert she got better—the caress of his smile as he looked deep into her eyes.

It was as if the light of the chandelier overhead had surged, it felt as if the sun had come out on the dark New York City night.

But then it faded and order returned to the sky.

'I should go,' Khalid said, for even from across the table she had got under his skin and he decided that their night was over. 'I'll have my driver take you to the airport.'

'Thank you,' Aubrey said.

She didn't mean it, though, for Aubrey did not want their time to end.

They walked out of the hotel restaurant and passed the bar and she looked in for a wistful moment. Brandy and the other women were around the piano and, boy, could they sing.

They were dressed now in sequins and kicking up their gorgeous long legs. Mom would have loved tonight, Aubrey thought. If only she had come, these women would have looked out for her mom as they would for her should she ask.

They were a sisterhood really.

'I am going to go up now,' Khalid said. 'Do you want to go in and join your friends?'

'No.' Aubrey shook her head as they resumed their walk through the foyer. The fact was she could go and join in and they would look after her. It actually didn't have to be the airport floor. 'Maybe.'

'My driver can take you any time you like,' Khalid offered.

He had kept his word, Aubrey realised. It had been dinner, that was all.

Except she didn't want it to be all.

It was Aubrey who wanted more and, despite what he thought her to be, it was everything else that he was—strong, sensual—that somehow made her feel safe.

Some day in the future Aubrey would know her first, and it was something she had silently dreaded.

Until now.

He could never imagine the wrestle that took place in her as they walked past the bar. Khalid could not know she was a virgin and how new this all felt to her.

All he responded to was the sensual air that surrounded them. 'I'll let the desk know now and then you can call for the driver whenever you are ready. Or,' he added, for he could resist her no more, 'you can come back to my suite.'

Aubrey stopped walking and as the sun returned to the night sky, she turned to face Khalid. Aubrey had never so completely met another's gaze before. If anything, she did her level best not to catch men's eyes, yet she held his, totally.

She saw the flecks of gold and the dark rim that seemed to hold inside it a circle of fire and he neither looked nor backed away from his invitation.

'I'd like that,' Aubrey said, for it was the truth. She wanted to be with Khalid, even if just for a night. She wanted him to be her first, yet he considered her way more experienced than she was. And if she told him her truth? Aubrey was rather certain that Khalid would politely wish her goodnight.

And so she lied by omission and chose not to tell Khalid her truth, and as he moved in to kiss her, his eyes still did not look away. Aubrey could feel the warmth of his mouth even before their lips had met and both closed their eyes as they did, for there could be no other way to sample such exquisite bliss. He kissed her so lightly that if she opened her eyes Aubrey was scared that he might have disappeared. That he might be a dream. Yet his lips pressed a little more firmly and parted hers.

Aubrey had truly never known a kiss, but even with nothing to compare it to she knew that his kiss was pure bliss. She could not have fathomed how, with such a gentle touch, her heart might tumble. It was as if he had found the weak spot within, the fracture line that, correctly tapped, might shatter her.

And he felt it too.

Tonight Khalid did not want the meaningless sex he survived on. He wanted to touch and to feel and for one night to fully indulge that. Today had been exceptionally hard—new grief and the resurgence of old grief had combined—but now there was a sweet reprieve and Audrey was the one he had found it with. She had consumed him on sight and it was a relief to finally hold her in his arms and kiss her lips as he wanted to.

But then he removed his kiss, and his hands held her hips as he made sure that Aubrey was clear as to the nature of his invitation.

'You understand that you won't be sleeping in the guest room?'

Oh, she did. Her lips ached for his and Khalid's hands on her hips were necessary for they held hers slightly back and prevented them from melding into his, as they felt inclined to do, and so she answered him honestly. 'I do.'

'Then come to bed.'

CHAPTER SIX

THE DOOR TO his suite closed behind them.

Then the bedroom door closed behind them too.

'All day I have wanted you,' Khalid said.

'I've wanted you too,' Aubrey admitted.

He held her head in his palms and kissed her eyes, her cheeks, her face, then her mouth. She could never have guessed just how rare such tenderness was for Khalid. He showered her with kisses, lowering his head as Aubrey resisted scaling his chest. And when their mouths met there was heady relief as she tasted the air that he breathed as their tongues slowly mingled.

His scent this close was intoxicating and she gave herself up to his kiss as he slipped down the zipper of her dress.

Aubrey felt the brush of air on her back as he exposed her skin then the light touch of his fingers tenderly exploring the notches of her spine. She *felt* in his kiss the brief irritation as he came to her bra strap, and then the whisper of relief from both of

them as he unclipped it and her skin was his to roam.
Khalid peeled down the straps of her dress and that
her bra was tatty didn't matter for it was a mere in-
convenient barrier that soon fell to the floor.

Her dress went with it and Khalid went to remove
his own clothes but Aubrey halted him.

'Let me,' she said, for she wanted finally to feel
the silk of his suit beneath her hands and to expose
the body that had transfixed her on sight. She pulled
the jacket down his shoulders and felt for a moment
his solid arms beneath the thick cotton of his shirt.
It was Aubrey who removed his cufflinks. A far
harder task than applying them for as she did his
hands toyed with her breasts, stroking and caressing
them. His palms were warm and his fingers a touch
rough, making it almost impossible to concentrate
on the task. Khalid lowered his head for a taste, and
the coolness of his tongue and the soft sucking had
her hold onto his shoulders merely to stay standing.

'Oh…' It was all she could manage, because at
the touch of his mouth she felt frantic and desperate
and even more so when he released her for the need
in her didn't dim.

Still dressed, he slid her knickers down and as she
dealt with his buttons, desperate to feel his skin, his
hand slipped between her thighs and she moaned at
the caress of his fingers there.

'Khalid,' she almost begged, for she wanted that
torso naked again, but she was sinking onto the bed.

He removed his shirt and she lay there watching

and fighting not to kneel up and to touch, but the reward was great for she feasted on the magnificent sight of him.

Then he undid his belt and she could see the bulge of his erection; it excited Aubrey more than it scared her. She had long thought of sex as a means to an end, she had never thought she might want another person so much.

He was so toned, so completely powerful that her breath caught in her throat. Aubrey had never seen a body so primed and so male. From her work she was used to seeing buffed, athletic men, but he really was something else. His stomach was flat and a thick snake of black hair drew the eyes down. He stripped to black boxer briefs that revealed thighs that were lean yet muscled and then Aubrey felt her bravado waver as he removed them.

Fear and want collided when she first saw him. Darker than the rest of him, erect and primed, she felt a lick of fear low in her belly and a thick stroke of desire between her thighs. She could not wing this, Aubrey knew, as his powerful form came over her as he knelt on the bed.

She lay on her back, still and now wary as his copper eyes explored her naked form. Aubrey wasn't shy with her body, yet he exposed places that no other had seen and he looked so hungrily and thoroughly that she felt the blush of heat between her legs.

She wanted.

And she did not want.

His hair, slicked back all day, fell forward now. Anticipation and fear rose in her as his mouth moved down and she let out a low moan as he kissed her stomach. She knew she had to tell him she was a virgin, for this was surely going to hurt.

Yet she did not want escape from this pleasure.

'Aubrey,' he told her as his tongue turned her stomach to tense knots and he kissed down to the blonde curls that encased her pink space, 'I have to taste you.'

And she had to tell him, yet his sinful lips were sublime.

He was slow and very thorough and when he needed to he parted her thighs some more, just to delve in fully.

And when she started to flail, when he knew she was near to coming, he tasted deeper and Khalid knew now why he so rarely indulged or let himself get close to someone. The mainland could declare war on Al-Zahan, there could be a coup at the palace, and all he would care for would be her pleasure and finishing this.

Her hips lifted but he held them down and he drank from her as her thighs tensed and her soft sighs turned to desperate moans.

Aubrey was lost, her fingers knotted in his hair, half dragging him off for it was so intense, and half pushing him in for more of the ecstasy he gave.

And wholly succumbing to his lips.

Aubrey had no breath in her and she dragged air in as his head rose from between her thighs.

She moved up to her elbows, trying to find her voice as he reached for protection.

'Khalid...' Her hand moved to his to halt him, but the feel of him on her fingers shot arrows of desire again to her groin and she closed her hand around him, just to stroke him, just to feel him.

He let out a primal, earthy groan at the light touch of her fingers and he resisted closing his hand over hers, for tonight he did not want rough.

She knelt up now, exploring him properly, stroking him, feeling him, feeling both sick and excited at the thought of him being inside her. 'I haven't done this, Khalid...' she said in a trembling voice, both worried about his reaction but also quivering with need.

'Shh,' he said, because he did not need her to play games. Khalid already wanted tender tonight. But then he looked from her inexpert hand to her eyes, and his heart was stripped bare when he saw that she did not lie.

A thousand questions exploded in his mind, and while he should possibly seek explanation, the truth was Khalid needed no answers now, his only need was for her.

He forgot about protection, he forgot Western rules, for in Al-Zahan they did not apply. In the harem he had discarded, there was no barrier to dull pleasure and tonight they might well have been be-

neath the stars on a sultry desert night as he kissed
her tense mouth until it was loose, sensual and his.

And Aubrey, who had expected confrontation or
accusations as she admitted her truth, understood
that she did not know this man, even as, honest now
and naked, they drew closer to bliss.

He kissed her until she was lying down again,
only this time he was atop her, and he came up on
his forearms as his tongue turned her molten.

Her hands held his shoulders and felt they were
solid, hard and strong, and though she sensed his
power, the fear of him being inside her had gone.

Until he almost was.

'It's going to hurt,' she anticipated as he held his
thick base and ran the head over her slick, hot opening.

'A minute of pain,' he said.

His deep voice next to her ear made her shiver and
when he first nudged in, Aubrey wanted to thrash
but his body pinned her, and she knew she could not
take a full minute of this.

'Soon,' Khalid said into the shell of her ear, 'I
give you pleasure.'

But first she had to live through that minute. It
was a pain she wanted, a moment she hadn't known
she needed, but as he squeezed in, her hips pulled
back and he smothered her scream with his mouth.

If she had not been lying down, Aubrey would
have fainted.

For Khalid it was an immeasurable bliss to sear

into her tight, wet space, and he had to fight with himself not to move. His body was ripped with both tension and a tug of affection, for he wanted her soothed, and he wanted her willing, so he held back from the desire to thrust and he kissed her back.

Her eyes were tightly shut as the hurt receded and Khalid pulled back, and then it returned as he pushed in. But it brought with the pain a new thick feeling of pleasure and Aubrey moaned.

He pulled almost out and then stabbed his heat in again and delivered more pleasure as the hurt receded in diminishing degrees as he moved within her.

She held his shoulders, pressing her fingers in and arching into him, and Khalid could not hold back any longer.

He was up on his forearms and moving so deep within her, spreading heat as she encased him. Her eyes opened and met his and her mouth reached up to kiss him and he let her, but then he removed his mouth for he could not hold back and Aubrey felt the change as he took her fast and hard.

'Kha-leed…' The word separated, the world separated, as he drove her to the edge, and when Aubrey came, when she stiffened and pulsed, when she made a cat-like cry, it finished Khalid and with a breathless shout he gave in to his own release.

She felt the rush of him and then he met her eyes and delivered slow, lingering thrusts as they both twitched in the last throes of pleasure.

He did not ask if it had hurt, for he had swallowed her scream.

Neither did he ask if her first time had been pleasurable for there was no question that it had been.

They kissed as if they had lain in this bed for far more than one night and between kisses he said things in Arabic that should never have been said.

'I want you in the morning. I want you in my desert bed. Already I am wanting you again.'

Aubrey bathed in his words, in his voice, in his touch, and when he rolled from her, he took her with him, and she curled into his arms.

And Khalid held her there, the rest of the world forgotten.

His country could have fallen and he would have cared not.

CHAPTER SEVEN

KHALID AWOKE LONG before dawn.

He had slept for an hour at best.

Just one stolen hour before thoughts had invaded and reality impinged, and immediately on waking Khalid knew he had gone too far. There was a very good reason that he chose more worldly partners. It didn't always work, of course, for they would fall in love and hope things might change, but he had the consolation of having said from the start, and had shown in his manner, that sex was all it was.

Last night he had crossed a line with Aubrey.

Had she told him earlier of her inexperience, he would never have brought her up here. He was more annoyed with himself than her. At his own assumptions. And at his lack of control.

Nothing could ever come of them and it was time to make that exceptionally clear.

'Aubrey?'

She woke to the deep sound of her name being called.

'You have to leave soon for your flight.'

She was twined into him, her leg over his, her face on his chest, and she lay there for a moment wondering about the questions that were surely to come. Except Khalid was not holding her and neither did he have any questions; instead, he told her how things would be. 'My driver will, of course, take you, so you have time for a shower.'

Had she not lain naked and wrapped around him, he might just as well have been the front desk, calling and reminding her of the time.

'Is that it?' Aubrey said as she removed herself from him and sat up in the bed. Khalid lay there, the arm closest to her behind his head, and he did not meet her eyes. 'The niceties are over?'

'I apologise,' Khalid rather sarcastically responded. 'Would you like me to have breakfast sent up?'

'Don't bother,' Aubrey said. She flounced to the shower and Khalid saw the blood on the sheets and, yes, he was angry.

Khalid was angry with himself, furious at his lapse and that he had brought the ways of home to this world, for he was well aware that he had not used protection. For a while last night it hadn't mattered, he had thought of her in his desert bed where the problems of this world did not apply.

Except Khalid had rejected the harem and though last night he had been tempted, he did not want that for Aubrey. He would speak to her when she came out about the morning-after pill. It was not a con-versation he had ever expected to have, for Khalid always took care.

Aware that he hadn't last night, Khalid decided to show care in the only way he knew and reached for the money clip beside the bed. He went to remove some notes but then stuffed the lot, diamond and all, into her purse.

And she saw…

Aubrey hadn't lingered in the shower and now stood, wrapped in a towel, as he sullied everything beautiful about last night.

'I really wish you hadn't done that…' she said in a shaken voice, and watched his naked back and shoul-ders tense as he realised she was there.

It didn't soften his stance, though. 'And I really wish that you hadn't pretended you knew what you were doing when you came up here last night.'

'Oh, so you'd have preferred a hook-up?'

'Yes,' Khalid said, for they were far less compli-cated. 'Tell me, Aubrey, are you on the Pill?' She didn't answer, which Khalid took as a no. 'There is a pill you can take—'

'I do know,' she snarled. 'It's fine, I am on the Pill.'

'Why?' Khalid said, feeling trapped and confused, rare for him, because everything he had assumed about Aubrey had been wrong, and everything he now felt about her was wrong by his country's stan-dards. 'What are you on the Pill for, or is that another of your lies?'

She could have told him it helped for performing, but the truth was she was as regular as a Swiss watch and instead she told him the truth. 'Because my mom made sure I was on it.' Aubrey could feel salty tears at the back of her throat because, while she loved her mom, that she turned a blind eye to where the money came from hurt very much.

And so did the warning in his next words—'Aubrey, you do *not* want to be pregnant by me.'

'You should have thought of that before.'

'I wasn't exactly thinking,' Khalid snapped, but then reminded himself that she could not possibly understand the folly of last night. His father had more bastards than Khalid could keep count of and certainly his father did not keep count of them. The children born from the harem were *nothing* to a prince or a king, and having seen first-hand the hurt it caused, Khalid did not want that for Aubrey. 'Had I been thinking then we wouldn't be in this mess.'

'Mess?' Aubrey checked, and he let out a mirthless laugh.

She couldn't believe the change in him. Last night he had been passionate, thoughtful and kind. Now it felt as if she were looking at a complete stranger and she just wanted to get away. 'I'll get my things.'

'Please do.'

She brushed past him and in the bathroom quickly dressed, not in the black dress but in the denim skirt and loose top she had changed out of at the airport, and she pulled on her sandals.

Back to the old Aubrey, she thought as she looked in the mirror.

But not quite, for last night had taught her a lot. And so, before she left, Aubrey took the money from her purse and the diamond clip too, and placed them on the bedside table.

'Take the money.' Khalid said. 'I can afford it.'

'You can't afford me, Khalid.' And she told him a truth. 'I refuse for last night to have made me a whore.' Aubrey tossed her purse over her shoulder and headed to the door, but before she left she said one more thing. 'I knew that you thought I was,' she admitted. 'When you asked about me and Jobe.'

'Then why act so hurt now when I do the right thing and pay you?'

'I'm not acting. I'm hurt because I honestly thought that last night was something more. I wasn't expecting for ever, but I wasn't expecting to be paid for my services either. I'll tell you something, Khalid—the working women I know take time off for their own sex lives. They're allowed a bit of romance too. God knows, they deserve it.'

Aubrey took the elevator and then walked briskly through the foyer.

It was empty in comparison to last night, but there were a few people milling around.

She passed the restaurant where they had dined—

now preparing for breakfast. Past the bar where Brandy and friends had sung for Jobe, but it was all closed now.

She paused for just a second, standing on the very spot they had first kissed, at the very place she had made her decision to go to his suite, and willed herself to regret her choice.

But she did not.

Up until this morning the time spent with Khalid had been the very best moments of her life.

Aubrey stepped out into the cold morning air. It was a beautiful day in New York City, yet it felt as if her heart had been cut out by his cold indifference. She had no idea how to get to the underground, but right now she just needed to put as much distance as she could between herself and Khalid.

'Aubrey!'

Khalid's shout was one of relief when he caught sight of her.

He had regretted his attitude even before the door had closed and he had hurriedly dressed, grabbing his phone to summon his driver should she already be gone.

Then he'd caught sight of her and the relief he felt sounded in his voice.

She stiffened but did not turn; instead, she walked on briskly and he ran to catch up, catching her arm, as he again called her name and then added. 'Don't go like this.'

'You want smiles?' Aubrey shouted, and then she

gave him one. The biggest, showiest smile that she could fake, and as she shrugged off his arm Aubrey blew him a kiss. 'Is that better?' She would cry later but right now she fought for pride.

'Aubrey,' he said. 'I apologise.'

His voice wasn't humble, his apology was bold and clear and deep, and something inside told her this was rare.

It was.

Khalid never, ever truly apologised. And it wasn't all due to his status. He ensured that he was never close enough to anyone that he might hurt.

But he had hurt her.

'Can we talk?' he asked.

'No,' Aubrey said, though she wanted to, she truly wanted to understand how in the space of a couple of hours—hours spent lying with each other and not apart—so much had changed. 'I've a flight to catch.'

'My driver—'

'The same driver that you offered me last night?' Aubrey sneered. 'Thanks, but I think I'll make my own way.'

But then she looked at Khalid. Really looked at the man who stood in front of her.

Yesterday he had been utterly groomed but now he stood in hastily pulled-on clothes. His white shirt was crumpled and barely done up and while he wore dress shoes, this morning they came with no socks.

He looked as dishevelled as she felt.

And he would not simply let her go. 'Aubrey, I will sort out another flight, this minute, just don't walk away. There is something I have to explain.'

After a moment she nodded, because that was what hope did.

Stupid, blind hope.

And so, instead of slapping his cheek and waving down a cab, just to get away, Aubrey let him take her arm and guide her across the street and towards the park. He bought coffee for them and on the way they sat on the bench, looking at the early morning joggers and the start of another New York day.

Aubrey assumed she was about to be told he had a wife, or perhaps given another reminder to take her Pill.

Her assumptions didn't come close to the truth.

'Last night should not have happened for many reasons. The main one being that I am royal.'

The bench didn't disappear from beneath her, but she held onto it with one hand just in case. 'Royal?'

'I am the Crown Prince of Al-Zahan.'

And she loathed that she couldn't nod with understanding but instead had to ask, 'What does that even mean?'

He had been told what it meant from a gilded cradle, and now he said it out loud on a park bench. 'I will be King.'

She watched a runner glide by as surely as that tiny kernel of hope slipped away. 'Do you want to be?' she asked, but her voice was on autopilot, the question more a statement.

Until he answered.

'Want is the only luxury denied to me.'

Aubrey swallowed on an empty throat.

'Needs can be met,' Khalid said, then turned and looked at her. 'And I hoped that you would suffice.'

Aubrey sucked in a breath because the words that he said sounded like an insult but his voice was laced with rawness and there was tenderness in his eyes. 'I didn't suffice?'

'No, for you made me want more.'

Aubrey suppressed a cry of frustration, for she didn't understand. She wanted to stamp her sandaled feet on the ground for he made no sense.

Yet deep down she understood.

She looked at the fresh new leaves that caught in the morning breeze and the tiny buds beside them, and she looked at a pinkish sky that hadn't yet learnt how to be blue.

But was *burning* itself to be.

There was *still* want.

'Last night *was* something more,' Khalid admitted. 'I wanted you, no matter the profession I thought you were in, but I was reckless too.'

'We both were,' Aubrey said, 'but it's fine, like I said, I'm covered.' She tried to lighten things a touch. 'I shan't create a scandal.'

'It would be more than a scandal, it would be unprecedented.'

Aubrey frowned, not understanding what he meant.

'Things are very different where I am from,' Khalid said. 'I go back there this evening. I doubt I shall be back in the States for a very long time.'

'Why?'

'I am assuming more duties at home,' Khalid said. 'My choice. There are things that need to be done, and I have fought hard to do them.'

'Like the hotel?'

'Yes.' Khalid nodded. 'It is a very rich country but the wealth stays too much in the palace, and it needs to trickle down. The hotel helps with that, it provides work and new openings. I cannot change much more from here, though I still hope to come back now and then.'

Aubrey swallowed, and her heart started thumping, not quite sure herself if his returning to America might include her, but then Khalid spoke on.

'One of the conditions of my assuming a more prominent role is that I marry and produce heirs. An amulet is being selected and the goldsmith will soon appear on the dome at the palace...' Khalid knew she could not understand that and he chose not to explain it. He could not look over as he spoke. 'I am expected to take a suitable wife.'

'Suitable?'

'Chosen by my father,' Khalid said. 'Where I come from there are many rules that you would not understand. Some are beautiful, some I am trying to change, and there are some that are non-negotiable. I have resisted marrying…'

'Why?'

'Because I don't like decisions to be made for me. But the fact is I cannot choose my bride.'

He was trying so carefully to tell her that they could never, ever be. Of course she was far from suitable, Aubrey already knew that, and so she said the hardest thing. 'I'm sure your father will do his best by you.'

And Khalid closed his eyes, for he had not expected her to defend his ways. But she was also wrong, for the King would not take Khalid's heart or mind into consideration. It would be decided on precious stones, armies and oil. 'Last night was a lapse.'

'Aren't you allowed sex out of wedlock?'

'Of course I am. I can have a harem but I disbanded it…'

'Why?'

Khalid didn't answer.

'Why?' she asked again.

'You are persistent.'

'When I choose to be.' Aubrey smiled and then she blinked, for she chose to be persistent only with Khalid. Even with her mom and those closest to her, Aubrey kept a shield between herself and them.

She wanted to know as much about Khalid as she could.

While she still could.

'Tell me,' Aubrey said, 'why did you disband your harem when surely it's every man's fantasy?'

'My father kept a harem—he still does—but that he did so while married hurt my mother in many ways. A harem is not just for sex, but for conversation and recreation too. My mother was in a very lonely, unhappy marriage. Her children, she said, were her only joy.'

'She had four?' Aubrey checked, thinking back to their conversation last night.

'Yes, but she died just after giving birth to the twins. My mother said to me that being the wife of a king was the biggest mistake of her life. She had been a princess in her own country and her father allowed her to come here to America as they waited to see the bride my father would choose. Within an hour of his decision she was on a plane and married the next day, and from then on she lived a lonely life.'

'Well, I hope you treat your wife better.'

'I shall, though a king cannot get emotionally involved with anyone.'

'You mean anyone other than your wife?'

'No, I mean with anyone,' Khalid reiterated.

'Why?'

Khalid didn't answer. He had neither the time nor inclination for a history lesson and certainly he did not want to pull rank. 'Now, I must sort out your flight for you. What time suits? I can have Laisha, my secretary, arrange a flight immediately or for later in the day. I am heading there late this afternoon.'

'Late afternoon works fine for me.'

It was all very efficient and soon her flight had been arranged and, with the time difference, she would be home by nine.

'I can still work tonight.' Aubrey smiled and then added, 'I do some trapeze—well, I do a lot of things, but I have a long shift tonight.'

'Aubrey, I want you to take the money,' Khalid said, 'not for last night, but for the nights to come. I know you are struggling.'

'How do you know?'

'Because you were going to sleep on the airport floor, because…' he did not want to mention that he knew where she lived, or that the clothes she wore… 'Aubrey, please take it.'

'I won't.' Aubrey was adamant. She would let nothing taint last night, but she offered a concession. 'Though you *can* buy me breakfast.'

Khalid did, although not back at the hotel.

Instead they had *churros* bought from a cart, and more coffee, of course, and walked and talked.

'Can you tell me why you were there yesterday?' he asked, not because of his allegiance to the Devereuxes. He really was too royal to gossip or reveal information, but he wanted to know. 'What did Jobe mean to you?'

'He used to have a thing with my mom.' There, she had said it. 'Do with that what you will.'

'I'm not going to say anything to Ethan.'

'I hope not,' Aubrey fretted, already feeling guilty for telling him, but the truth, or a small part of it, was surely better than Khalid thinking she had been some sort of paid date for Jobe. 'My mom will freak if she finds out I've said anything.'

'Aubrey.' Khalid could see she was worried. 'This shall go no further. You don't have to say any more.'

Yet she wanted to. 'I don't know how Mom and Jobe started but it became more than just an occasional thing.'

'How long were they together?' Khalid asked.

'Years.' Aubrey thought back. 'From when I was about ten. He treated her like gold when he was with her, and me.' She told him about the violin and music lessons and the holidays they had taken too, but it was the violin that interested him most.

'You play the violin?' Khalid asked, and they stopped walking and he turned and faced her.

She nodded and he watched the colour spread on her cheeks.

'I used to be really good.'

'Used to be?' he checked. 'Aubrey, you're twenty-two, nearly twenty-three, so *used to be* can't be that long ago.'

'How do you know my age?'

Khalid didn't answer. Realising what he had said, his world was silently rocked for he was never indiscreet. Ever. But talking like this with Aubrey did not feel like an indiscretion. It was one, of course, by the standards he set himself, yet to reassure Aubrey, he moved the bar.

'It's not what you think,' she blurted out.

'I don't know what to think, Aubrey.'

'Jobe gave me money to study music, and instead…' She was starting to panic and was too scared of the truth to finish.

'Aubrey, tell me…'

'So that you can tell them?'

'No, so that you can feel better.'

'How is telling you going to help?'

Except it did.

'I spent it on my mom. She'd broken up with Jobe because of Chantelle, but Mom said they would get back together, that he'd marry her, but then came the fire. She was at a party, and her costume caught alight. Well, when I say a party, she was with clients…' He really was the kindest man, because he must have heard her shame and instead of recoiling or judging he took her hand as they walked. 'She suffered burns to her face, neck and chest.'

'Did Jobe know about the fire?'

'No, and Mom didn't want him to,' Aubrey said. 'She wanted him to remember her as she was.'

'So he sent you money each month.'

'To study music. When he broke things off with Mom, before he left he spoke to me and said that I should try and make something of myself. And I wanted to…'

'But then the fire happened?'

Aubrey nodded. 'I've been taking money by deception…'

'What makes you think that?'

'The Internet,' she admitted.

Khalid smiled and he gave her hand a squeeze. 'Aubrey, Jobe sent you money, I would expect it was to assuage his guilt for his treatment of you and your mom.'

'Guilt?' Aubrey frowned. 'He was wonderful, though.'

'He was also fallible. I am sure he enjoyed the times spent in Vegas but he was never going to marry your mom and, even if he did, it would be on impulse and something he would make go away.'

'No,' she still insisted, but though he broke her heart as he held her hand, when she went to pull hers away, he just held it tighter. 'Things got better when Jobe came into Mom's life.'

'Better?' Khalid checked. 'How?'

'Well, there weren't...' Aubrey swallowed, not sure how to voice that once Jobe came on the scene there hadn't been an endless parade of men, as Jobe had insisted that her mom only see him. 'Are you saying he used her?'

'I am saying that Jobe was complex, and he had many sides. He was never going to give himself to one woman, even if he promised that one day he might.'

No, Aubrey wanted to say.

Except she didn't.

'My mom always wanted to go to a ball,' Aubrey said, and she felt Khalid look over as they walked. 'It was her dream. Well, apart from a big white wedding. You'd think, if he was never going to marry her, he could at least have given her that.'

Khalid chose to stay silent.

'She was just part of his harem, wasn't she?'

'I didn't say that.'

'No, I did. She was good for fun, and a laugh, and sex, but not good enough to be seen on his arm. Even on our holidays he wore a cap and shades…'

'Aubrey…'

'It's true,' Aubrey said, she could see it so clearly now. 'He didn't want her to change and to grow, he wanted to keep her exactly as she was.'

'Aubrey, we have so little time, can we stop speaking about your mom and Jobe?'

'But I'm not talking about them,' Aubrey said.

Khalid frowned, for perhaps he had misunderstood. 'What I'm trying to say—'

'Is that in a few months' time you'll be back in the States for a visit.' Aubrey finished his sentence for him. 'And perhaps we could get together then? That's what you're trying to say.'

'No,' Khalid said, and he turned her so that they faced each other; he took her cheeks in his hands. 'I am calling on every ounce of willpower I possess *not* to say that.'

She believed him, so much so that salty tears slid down her cheeks and met his warm fingers and she could actually see the battle in his eyes.

'The best I could offer you is to be my *ikbal*, and you don't want that.'

'I don't even know what it is.'

'The favoured one,' Khalid said, 'the chosen one.'

'But not the wife.' Aubrey said, understanding better now. 'It's one helluva offer, Khalid, but no.'

Even during the most difficult conversation she made him smile, but then Khalid was serious.

'I thought as much, and I am proud of you, for you deserve more and so does my future wife. Aubrey, I shall not call, and I shall not see you after today. I love my country and my people, but to make the changes that I want to…'

'You have to toe the line?'

'No,' Khalid said rather mysteriously. 'I have to appear to.'

He kissed her then, right there in the park, soft and strong, salty and sweet. Her mouth knew his now and she closed her eyes to savour the bliss, and almost wished he had not run after her.

Almost wished she didn't know that they could never, ever be.

And then, because he had to, Khalid let her go.

'I need to get back to the hotel and get changed,' Khalid said, still holding her close. 'I am due to meet with my brothers and sisters, but if you wait in my suite we can talk some more afterwards.'

'Won't they come up to your suite?'

'No, we are meeting for high tea, but it will just be for an hour.'

'Ah, yes, you keep things formal.'

'You said you liked that,' Khalid pointed out.

'Yes, but…' She looked beyond him and then up—the sun was creeping across the sky, Central Park smelled of spring and she wanted this day to last for ever, but more than that she wanted this formal man to know, even for a short while, how much fun life could be. 'Why do you have to get changed? Why don't you just have a picnic with them out here?' Aubrey said. 'I'll wait in your suite, but have the hotel bring a picnic out here.'

'No,' He dismissed her suggestion with a flick of his hand. 'I need to discuss their school reports and such things.'

'And you can't do that outside?'

'It is already awkward enough,' Khalid said. 'My sister has discovered make-up!'

Aubrey laughed.

Khalid did not.

'There will be no picnic,' Khalid said. 'We have important things to discuss.'

'So did we,' Aubrey said, refusing to give in. 'And wasn't that difficult conversation made so much easier by being out in the open?'

'Perhaps,' Khalid conceded. 'But we are not a family who picnics.'

'Why?'

He was about to remind her to stop questioning him, except he liked the challenge of it.

'Khalid, spend some time with your family in the sun.'

He saw again the pleading in her blue eyes and it

was even more insistent than last night. The halva ice cream had been a game, but the look she gave now was an imperative plea.

And one he heeded.

'On one condition,' Khalid said. 'Would you care to join us?'

Aubrey would know this day too.

CHAPTER EIGHT

KHALID'S SIBLINGS WERE GORGEOUS.

And mightily surprised when their older brother met them in the foyer looking slightly the worse for wear and introduced them to his blonde, denim-skirted friend.

Khalid arranged the picnic with the concierge and soon they were back in the park.

Hussain, at sixteen, was awkward and shy; he had a delicate soul and a dreamy nature and from all Aubrey could glean Khalid was fiercely protective of him.

Abbad, at fourteen, was aloof and rather more like Khalid. Nadia was exuberant and pretty and so excited to be out in the sun as the waiters spread the rug on the grass.

It was a picnic, though not like any Aubrey was used to for the food had been prepared by a chef and the plates were china.

'It was Aubrey's idea to eat outside,' Khalid explained once they were seated.

'Where are you from?' Abbad asked.

'Vegas,' Aubrey said, and ate a tiny sandwich. 'I'm headed back there tonight.'

Yes, it was a little strained and awkward, but what Aubrey did not know was that it was by far less strained and awkward than it usually was.

Khalid asked about their school work and it was clear to Aubrey that, despite austere appearances, he cared deeply for them—he had agreed to eat out here after all.

'I want to do drama,' Hussain said, 'but I don't think that would go down well with the King.'

'If you keep doing English,' Khalid responded, 'I will tell him that drama is a compulsory unit. Don't worry, he leaves most of that to me.' He turned to his sister. 'What about you, Nadia?'

'I'm a straight A student.' Nadia shrugged, concentrating on selecting a strawberry rather than meeting her eldest brother's eyes. 'My report will be excellent, just you wait and see.'

'I'm sure your grades will be, but I received a phone call to say you have been sent out of class twice now for wearing too much make-up.'

Aubrey watched as Nadia nervously swallowed and still did not look up. Khalid did not seem cross, but he was serious and soon she understood why.

'I have asked that they do not put it in your report,' Khalid said. 'But, Nadia, why would you risk it? The King would see you wearing make-up as a further reason to bring you home.'

'I was trying to look natural,' Nadia said. 'I'm

just terrible at it. I watched some tutorials online but when I tried to copy them I ended up with stripes…'

Aubrey looked over and saw Khalid's non-comprehending frown. Clearly, he had no idea about make-up, or contouring, or just how badly you could get it all wrong at fourteen.

'I was the same,' Aubrey admitted. 'I only know how to apply stage make-up. I went and had a make-over yesterday.' She told Nadia about Vanda, and how kind she had been. 'She knew I wasn't going to buy anything but she gave me loads of tips…'

'Why wouldn't you buy the make-up?' Nadia asked.

'Nadia.' Khalid stepped in and saved Aubrey from explaining something that Nadia, with a very generous monthly allowance, could never understand. 'Go and see Vanda, rather than looking things up online, and tell her that Aubrey sent you.'

'Oh, I doubt she'd remember me.' Aubrey flushed.

'Of course she will remember you,' Khalid said.

And so too would he.

He looked at his siblings, more relaxed than he had ever known them, as was he. Instead of sitting in a formal restaurant, he lay on his side on the grass, propped up on his elbow and chatting more easily. And for Aubrey, who had made this possible, he had one small surprise. 'Aubrey was upset last night,' Khalid said to his siblings.

'No, I wasn't.' Aubrey frowned.

'She was upset because she has never had halva ice cream before and I didn't allow her to try any of mine.'

'That's mean.' Nadia smiled.

'Then it's time to rectify it,' Khalid said.

Sure enough, they were being served the coveted ice cream in bowls and Aubrey laughed so much as she took her first taste.

'What do you think?' Khalid asked.

'It's delicious,' Aubrey said and then met his eyes for a private smile. 'I would still have preferred to try it last night.' For surely it would have tasted even better if it came from his spoon?

He saw that private smile and were it possible he would whisk her upstairs for a private tasting right this minute, but it was rare family time now. And that time was to prove more important than Khalid could have envisaged.

'I sneak halva when I am at home,' Nadia said. 'And when I am cross…' She stopped herself from continuing and Khalid frowned, for he did not understand.

'I used to do that,' Aubrey said with a smile, and Khalid looked over to where she sat. Her legs were tucked behind her and the breeze caught her golden hair; without make-up she looked terribly young.

Yet she was wise, Khalid realised, for she made a guarded Nadia smile with what she said. 'I used to take cookie dough ice cream from the fridge. I would tear a chunk off and put it in a bag I kept right at the back of the ice box and I would add to it.'

'Why?' Khalid asked.

'So that when I was upset I had plenty of cookie dough ice cream to make me feel better.'

Khalid gave a brief shake of his head, for it made no sense to him, but then his sister spoke. 'When I am cross with the King, I eat halva in my suite…'

He looked at Aubrey, whose eyes seemed to be urging him not to let this conversation go.

'We all get cross with him,' Khalid gently said to his sister.

'Even you?'

'Yes.' Khalid nodded and he turned again to Aubrey. 'Nadia is a lot like our mother, a little impetuous and argumentative at times, and though that is a good thing, it also makes the King cross.'

'You said that I look like her.' Nadia pushed for more conversation about her mother.

'Which you do,' Khalid agreed.

'Khalid?' Nadia's voice had gone husky and Aubrey looked over to where the young girl sat. 'Did she ever see us?' Her face was flushed and her eyes were filling with tears.

'Yes,' Khalid said. 'She held you both for two full minutes and she said her family was complete, that she had the most beautiful children. And she kissed you both, and she asked for Hussain to come and meet his new brother and sister.'

Nadia was crying and Abbad stared ahead, but Hussain sat upright, his eyes narrowed. He rarely challenged anyone but on this day he did.

'You don't know this. You just say these things, why?'

'I *do* know this,' Khalid calmly answered. 'Because after her funeral I went and spoke with the medical staff who had been with her, and I found out all I could.' At the time it hadn't been for his brothers and sisters; he had wanted to know about his mother's last moments for himself. The time was right to share them now. 'She was happiest when with her children, I promise you that, and she would speak of you to me. Hussain is so funny, she would say, she was so proud of you…'

Aubrey watched as a tear spilled down Hussain's cheek and as he went to fiercely wipe it away, Khalid caught his brother's hand and held it and as Hussain wept he told them some more, and like thirsty sponges they soaked it up.

How Dalila had loved to sing.

That one night she had been found in the kitchen, making bread the way it was made in her own country.

And he told them how she had adored the history of Al-Zahan and had been a collector of the amulets given to newlywed couples to promote fertility.

'Her collection is on loan to a gallery off Fifth Avenue,' Khalid said. 'Go look at it when you miss her.' He looked at Aubrey, who had made this all possible. For, yes, it was easier to say these things in the warm sunshine, but it was also easier to speak like this, with her near.

Khalid did not know why.

'She loved you all so much, and if you want to know more about her, ask me.'

They did.

And then they spoke about other important things.

'I cannot be King,' Hussain said urgently. 'Khalid, I *cannot* marry.'

'I know,' Khalid said gently.

'You don't understand. I *cannot* make heirs.'

There was a dart of tension as Nadia and Abbad shared a glance. Aubrey saw it and guessed they had long known Hussain's secret, and she looked at Khalid, who still held his brother's hand.

'Hussain, you are not next in line—that is me.'

'And you refuse to marry. Now he threatens that if you don't comply then there are two more sons who can step in...'

'I don't want it to fall to me,' Abbad said, and Khalid could hear the note of fear in his voice, for, though similar in nature to Khalid, he had not been raised to be King and had known a lot of freedom.

Hussain spoke. 'There is no way out. If you don't comply with his rule, then it falls to us. If we don't step up then Al-Zahan falls to the mainland. You have to marry, Khalid,' Hussain said urgently. 'And you have to have a son.'

'Hussain,' Khalid responded in an even tone, 'I shall not marry because my father tells me to, and neither shall I marry just because you want me to. Certainly, I am in no rush to produce an heir. I have no interest in fatherhood.'

'But—' Hussain attempted.

'No buts,' Khalid said. 'I have listened to you,

now listen to me. I have told the King that for the next year my focus is on my country, and also the new hotel...'

'*Then* you will marry.'

'Hussain,' Khalid warned, refusing to be pushed. 'I shall look for a solution...' Khalid faltered, when he so rarely did, but it dawned on him that there could be no solution for him.

Khalid knew then why today was made easier with Aubrey there.

Life felt better with her by his side.

It was a revelation, for Khalid had never, for a second, expected love to enter his life. And there was nothing to mark the moment that it did. Children ran, parents chased, and his brothers and sister waited for him to go on.

Not Aubrey.

She had put on her shades and was lying back on the grass, appearing to enjoy the midday sun.

But she wasn't.

It killed her to hear him talk of marriage and heirs and for them to speak of a world she would never see and one where she could never belong.

And she lay back and closed her eyes on tears and listened as Khalid reassured his siblings, but his words did not comfort her. 'You have to trust that I shall strive for a solution that takes care of everyone. Life will be good, you will see.'

Khalid himself could not see a solution, though.

It was a long picnic, and there were fond goodbyes, and as she hugged Nadia and even the brothers, it hurt that she would never see them again.

And when they were gone, when she and Khalid were alone again in his suite, there was an even fonder goodbye. They made love because there was no tomorrow and then showered together. And when their time was up, never had being heir to the throne felt more of a burden to Khalid.

'I will call the butler to pack—'

'Don't,' Aubrey interrupted him, because she could not bear the sensual haven they had created to be disturbed. The drapes were closed across the entire suite, the bed unmade, and they stood in the bathroom dripping wet from a long, steamy shower.

And now it must all come to an end.

Khalid wrapped a towel around his hips and headed out to summon the necessary staff to organise his leaving New York as Aubrey stood and gripped the sink, trying to tell herself she could say goodbye without crying. Trying to convince herself that one night, one day was surely better than none.

She reached for a comb, his silver comb, anything other than focus on their parting, but as she did so she saw the small silver bottle with Arabic engravings. Ready for distraction and not so worried about touching Khalid's things now, she unscrewed the lid, removed the small stopper and inhaled deeply.

Oh, that scent!

She took the stopper and dabbed it on her neck, her wrists...

'Aubrey?'

She smiled in the mirror when caught but Khalid was not smiling.

'You can't wear that...'

'I *have* to wear it,' Aubrey corrected. 'Let me have some.'

'That scent is not for anyone but me,' Khalid said, and he came up behind her. That scent had been designed for him, and only his future bride could wear it. He was not cross, for he had never expected her to understand the ways of Al-Zahan, and while he knew she meant no harm, the deeper truth was that he wished she could wear his scent.

His arms came either side of her and she held the bottle up high, though Khalid could easily reach it, he did not take it from her tight grip; instead, he lightly ran his fingers down her naked ribcage till, laughing, she released it.

He replaced the stopper and put the bottle back down on the bench and told a breathless and laughing Aubrey their new plans. Still behind her, he hooked his strong arms under hers. 'We have an hour.'

'But I'll miss my flight,' Aubrey said, watching his dark hands span her stomach.

'You're getting a later one.'

His fingers were kneading her stomach and she watched their darkness press into her pale flesh. She could feel the nudge of him behind her as relief washed through her that it wasn't yet goodbye.

'Let me have your scent,' Aubrey said as his hands

moved up to her breasts. She didn't want his money, she simply wanted something of his. 'I just want a keepsake…'

'Shh,' he said, and she could feel him harden and the rock of him in the small of her back. His hands sent tiny volts through her and his fingers stretched and rubbed her nipples to what felt like capacity, because she was filling up low in her stomach and pressing back into him.

He lowered his head and he kissed her neck and she felt as if she had a fever as he sucked on flesh between her neck and collarbone. Even as she went to lean forward he held her up against him.

One hand worked her breast and the other slid down and he found the spot that made her quiver at his cruelly slow beats of pressure…

'Khalid…' she said. He removed his finger and offered it to her mouth and she sucked on it, then he placed it back where it was urgently required.

His eyes were open, watching them both in the mirror, and though Aubrey had been doing the same, the pleasure was too exquisite and she closed them.

'Khalid, please.' She was asking him to push her forward, for him to take her from behind, to fill her, but he misinterpreted.

'You can't have the scent, Aubrey.'

It hadn't been what she'd meant, but, oh, to be denied while being held so close meant that now she really wanted it!

Hot and wet, she turned in his arms and her face was

buried in his chest and she inhaled his scent, and licked him and tasted him and her teeth grazed his flat nipples.

His hand came to push her head away, to push it down, for it was unbecoming in a prince to let her mouth linger there, and suck and taste till he was weak. Yet he did not push her head away.

Aubrey could feel the tension and hear his ragged breathing as she nipped him with her teeth. She knew not what she was doing, just that their pleasure was intense, and her mouth moved down. Licking and sucking his taut stomach, bending at her knees and just making out with the dark skin there as her hand slid between his thighs.

And she first tested her power on a very willing source. 'I *want* that scent, Khalid.'

He did not answer.

So she kissed just above his hipbone and his hand pushed on her scalp.

She kissed up, and heard his hiss of frustration as her tongue brushed his ribcage and she moved up to be kissed.

'I want it, Khalid...' Aubrey did. She didn't want money, she just wanted one little keepsake, to recall the scent that had turned her first to him. 'Please...' she begged.

He relented, but with compromise. 'Kneel for me, then.'

He was tall, so tall, but she pulled a towel under her knees and licked up his thighs, and then cupped his balls and held him. 'I don't know what to do.'

'Then practise.'

Aubrey did, tentatively at first, licking his soap-scented length, and then swirled her tongue round the head, scared she might hurt him.

'You won't,' he assured her as her mouth covered him and she took him in.

Aubrey held his hips and the rhythmic buck of him was her guide. His hands smoothed her hair from her face and then held it pleasantly taut. She was exquisitely turned on, the heat of him and the way he slowed her down at one point told her he was close.

'Aubrey…' He said her name and it sounded like a warning so she took him a little deeper than she had thought she would dare.

He made a low growly noise and then let out a curse as he lifted her head from him, and seeing him so aroused and shiny and close had her wonder why he'd stopped her, but as she went to lower her head and finish him, his hands went under her arms and Khalid lifted her onto the cold marble bench.

'I have to have you one more time…' Khalid said, and he roughly parted her legs and scooted her forward so Aubrey was on the edge.

He was thorough rather than urgent, for he positioned her exactly and, more than that, to her frustration he moved the shaving mirror.

'What are you doing?' Aubrey begged urgently, but Khalid refused to be rushed.

He returned to her his full attention and he fanned her damp curls and then stroked her for an indulgent moment before, very deliberately and very slowly, he entered her.

'Watch,' Khalid said.

'I can't,' Aubrey admitted, because her bottom was lifting off the marble and she was fighting not to come.

It was uncomfortable on the marble and she twisted a little but the grip of his hands on her hips did not let her move so she leant back onto the glass mirror, which was cold on her naked shoulders.

And then she found out why he had moved the shaving mirror for it was perfectly angled towards the sight of them. It felt like an out-of-body experience, feeling him while watching him glide in and out. She could see her swollen flesh and the veins on his thick, dark length. Her thighs started to tremble yet still he held them wide open.

'I can't…' Aubrey said, and even she didn't know what she meant by that.

'You can,' Khalid said, as if he understood her words.

He moved faster and held her tighter and Aubrey felt a shiver run through her and a scream build inside her. She could feel tears running down her flushed cheeks as he relentlessly moved within her.

'I can't,' she said again, and now understood her own meaning, because she just did not know how to feel this much in one moment.

How to give in to him while knowing in the next moment she had to let go of him for all time.

But then Khalid showed her how.

He let go of her hips and shot into her with a breathless shout, and the sound and feel of him dragged out her scream and she wrapped her legs around him and gave in. She came so deeply that it hurt but Khalid lifted her and she coiled around him, resting her head on his shoulder as he thrust the last into her.

And she did not want it to end.

Did not want those flickers to be fading.

She felt dizzy and bereft when he slowly let her down and not even the tender slow kiss they shared could make this better.

'I don't want to go home,' she admitted, with her face pressed to his naked chest.

Come with me, Khalid wanted to say. *Come to Al-Zahan and be my lover for ever, my* ikbal, *my confidante and friend.*

But never his wife.

And so he peeled her from him. 'We must go.'

Two butlers came to pack up the suite but Aubrey could not bear to watch and instead headed down to the foyer to wait for him there.

And then Khalid's driver drove them to the airport and it was there that they said goodbye.

'Here,' Khalid said, and he took her hand and placed in it the silver bottle and closed her fingers around it. It was forbidden that she have it, of course, but he could not deny her the one thing from him she had asked.

'I hope they don't confiscate it.' Aubrey tried to make a joke and that squeezed his brutal heart.

God, but he loathed leaving her.

'What will you do?' he asked as he returned Aubrey to her life.

'What I always do,' Aubrey said. 'Survive.'

'No,' Khalid said, and pulled her back. 'You will strive.'

They shared one more long, lingering kiss, then it really was time for goodbye and all too soon Aubrey sat in her first-class seat and buried her face in the hot towel provided and fought hard not to cry.

Soon this feeling would pass, she told herself.

Soon it would hurt far less.

Khalid's plane had already commenced its long journey to Al-Zahan and he flew east over the Atlantic as Aubrey flew west for Vegas until they could not be further apart.

Oh, abnay alhabib... *I have fought for you to walk in the sun and laugh as I did.*

He finally had.

Now it was time to return to the desert.

And duty.

CHAPTER NINE

KHALID HAD TAUGHT Aubrey many things.

About her body, of course, yet he had taught her far more about herself.

Turning down that money had been harder than Khalid could know, but Aubrey was so glad that she had.

She knew now that history would *not* be repeating itself and she would *strive* for more.

Aubrey just worked harder. She worked in the casinos on the Strip during the day and headed for Downtown Vegas by night. Wearing white platform boots and a tiny red costume and big red wig, she performed with two other girls, dancing to keep warm on cold desert nights and having her photo taken with tourists.

And she had a secret too.

Every week, unbeknownst to family and friends, she knocked on an old man's door.

David had advertised online and it had taken all her courage to call him and eventually go to his home.

And, contrary to what it looked like, it was David who charged her for the hour-long session!

Aubrey took the money she had held back from her tips, held back from paying bills or her mom's meds, or a coffee to keep awake and warm and somehow invested in her dream.

For an hour, one precious hour a week, she had a violin lesson.

Aubrey used one of David's practice violins, as she didn't want to arouse the suspicion of her mom, but she used the violin Jobe had given her, and a silencer, to practise at home.

She looked within and dug deep, and while there were times she felt guilty about the money she was investing in hopes and dreams of a better future, Aubrey justified it.

For just as she paid for her mom's scripts to be filled, music was *her* medicine.

And she did all this while missing Khalid so much.

Soon she would get over him, Aubrey told her aching heart. If she threw herself into work, into her music, the craving would surely fade.

It didn't.

Oh, the girls were nice and the music so loud and the crowds so big that she wasn't much able to think.

That came later, generally around three in the morning when the street started to empty out and Aubrey changed into leggings and a thin oversized jumper to take the BHX bus home and it was then the ache of missing Khalid took its grim hold.

On this night, though, before she took the BHX, she stopped at the drug store to pick up her mom's meds. One of the scars on her mom's neck had become inflamed and was causing her a lot of pain, and yesterday Aubrey had taken her to a clinic. Never fun, as her mom loathed going out, or being seen, but she had covered herself with scarves and a hat and glasses and had finally got the wound looked at.

'You've taken these before?' the pharmacist checked as he dispensed the meds.

And Aubrey nodded, too weary this morning to explain they were for her mom. She just wanted to pay and get home to bed.

'You know not to drive or drink alcohol with them?' the very thorough pharmacist checked, holding up the pain pills.

'Sure.' Aubrey nodded. She just wanted to get away.

'And that contraception might not be effective with these?' He held up the antibiotics.

Aubrey swallowed.

No, she had not known that. Usually she just zoned out at the pharmacy's spiel, or said that her mom had taken them many, many times before. But these were the tablets she had taken for her ear infection. Aubrey hadn't gone to the clinic to get it checked, she had just taken some of her mom's bountiful supply. 'What do you mean, not effective?' she asked, trying to keep the urgency from her voice.

'Don't rely on the Pill when you're taking these,' the pharmacist said, and then smiled. 'Wrap it up.'

Only they hadn't.

As she lined up to pay, Aubrey tried hard to ignore the pharmacist's words, but she felt as if a hand was choking her throat.

She'd know if she was pregnant, surely?

Yes, she'd been sick a few times, but an internet search had told her she could blame that on her ear infection.

Aubrey was brilliant at avoiding paying for a doctor's consult for herself!

Yet she could not avoid this.

It had been six weeks since she had slept with Khalid and, no, she hadn't had a period, but that was because she'd been continually taking her Pill.

Aubrey threw in a home pregnancy test to be sure, or rather to reassure herself.

Only it didn't.

Aubrey sat on the edge of her bed and idly plucked the strings of her gorgeous violin. It was something that she did when restless or nervous and this morning Aubrey was the latter. The soft notes that she played stopped as she watched the indicator change, and every hope she'd ever had about getting out of here, every dream she'd had about her music, her life, blew away.

And she heard again the warning in Khalid's voice as he'd said, 'Aubrey, you do *not* want to be pregnant by me.'

What had he meant?

Khalid was a royal prince, and a future king.

She lay on her bed, staring up at the ceiling and wondering what on earth to do. Did she tell him? And if she did, then what? Her mind was swirling, turning, torn and confused.

Khalid had said that for her to be pregnant would be unprecedented, but surely there were strategies for dealing with all eventualities.

She could hear her mom was up and Aubrey hid the pregnancy test—just in time because her mom came in. 'Did you get my pills? Stella asked, by way of good morning.

'You're supposed to knock,' Aubrey reminded her.

'I did knock, you just mustn't have heard me.' Stella said, and came and sat on the bed. 'You've been crying.'

Had she?

'I'm just tired.'

'Are you sure it's just that?'

Aubrey nodded.

She wasn't so much scared of telling her mom she was pregnant, more she rather knew what her response would be.

She did not know what to do, and so for the next few weeks Aubrey held it all in, tucking herself into her tight costumes, day after day, and night after night, but her nerve had left her, and she was, for the first time, hesitant on the trapeze.

It did not go unnoticed.

'A five-year-old could have done that routine,' she was told by Vince when she stepped down.

'I'm just a bit off tonight.'

'Then lift your game or go home.'

Aubrey couldn't lift her game. She was suddenly scared she might fall, so she went home.

Her mom and Aunt Carmel were sitting on the porch by the time she got back. Aunt Carmel had red hair dye on and a towel around her shoulders and gave Aubrey a surprised smile. 'You're early.'

'Yep.' She did not want to explain in front of her aunt why she was home.

'There's some dinner,' her mom said. 'Have something to eat before you head out.'

'I'm not working any more tonight,' Aubrey said. 'I'm going to bed.'

She simply could not face it tonight so she lay on her bed and listened as Aunt Carmel and her mom chatted outside about the good old days, as they always did, but they didn't speak for so long tonight.

Soon they said goodnight and her mom came inside and then opened Aubrey's bedroom door.

'Can't you knock?' Aubrey snapped.

'Sorry,' she conceded. 'Aubrey, what's wrong?'

'Vince sent me home. He said a five-year-old could do my routine.'

'Then get back there and show him what you're made of!'

'I can't,' Aubrey said, 'because I'm scared of falling.'

'But you've never been scared before.'

Aubrey took a deep breath. 'I've never been pregnant before!'

'Oh, Aubrey…' her mom said in a sad, resigned voice. 'You could have told me.'

'I'm telling you now.'

'How far along are you?'

'Three months.' Aubrey lay with her eyes closed, knowing what was to come.

'You need to get onto it,' Stella said. 'You're getting to the stage where no doctor will want to touch you…'

Her eyes snapped open. 'Is that all you have to say?'

'Come off it, Aubrey.' Stella wasn't cross. 'What else is there to say?' Then she thought of something. 'Do you know who the father is?'

Aubrey said nothing and it broke her heart that her mom took her silence to mean no.

She lay with arms folded as her mother spelled out their rather precarious situation. 'You're not going to be able to work for much longer and we're barely getting by as it is…'

'And whose fault is that?' Aubrey said. 'You haven't worked in four years.'

'No one's going to employ me looking like this. If it hadn't been for the fire Jobe would have…'

But she didn't want to hear her mom's fantasy about Jobe rescuing them played over and over so she interrupted the stream of might-have-beens with more practical solutions. 'You could work phones. Aunt Carmel told you she might be able to arrange that. You could get a housekeeping job at one of the hotels but, no, you sit in here taking your meds and moaning about money and do absolutely nothing to help yourself.' Aubrey could see her mother's aghast face as she jumped out of bed.

'Aubrey, I can't go out looking like this.'

'Can't or won't?' Aubrey shouted.

It was a row that had been coming for a long time. One that Aubrey had held back from having, as she didn't want to hurt her mom, but, hell, she was not giving up her baby. 'I'll be back working tomorrow night. I'll support myself, and my baby. And when I start to show *I'll* work the phones and *I'll* do house-keeping, but I am not killing my baby because *you* choose to sit here and let life pass you by.'

Aubrey pulled on some clothes and picked up her purse and walked out into the night. She walked and she sobbed and she *wanted* Khalid, but was terrified of what the consequences might be if he found out.

If anyone found out.

Would he insist that she get rid of it?

Or would he have some claim on her baby? Would it be taken away?

Aubrey wouldn't risk finding out.

If there was one good thing about this day and the terrible row with her mom, it had taught her one thing. She *wanted* her baby. Desperately.

And she would survive.

Hell, she wasn't the first single mom around here.

Though the first who'd borne the child of a prince, she was sure.

No one must know, Aubrey vowed. No one must ever know.

It was very late when she returned home, and Aunt Carmel was there with her mom.

'Here she is.' Aunt Carmel smiled.

'I've kept your dinner warm, go and sit down,' her mom said as Aubrey took a seat, and she was brought her dinner on a tray and made a fuss of. 'I'm sorry, Aubrey.'

'I know,' Aubrey said, she could see that her mom had been crying and knew this was hard on her. Not just the news of the baby but the harsh words that had been said too.

'It was just a bit of a shock. You know I hate how things have turned out. If there hadn't been that damn fire, well, Jobe and I...'

Aubrey closed her eyes.

She knew now that it wasn't the fire that had kept them apart.

And it wasn't even Chantelle.

Jobe had adored her mom, but it had been nothing more than an escape for him. Jobe had never been going to propose or marry her, or all the things her mom had dreamed, but Aubrey didn't crush her with that, for finally Stella Johnson was trying. 'I'm going to make some phone calls tomorrow, and see about getting some work. We'll be okay, you know that, Aubrey. We always have been.'

Yes, they had always been okay.

Sort of.

CHAPTER TEN

AAYIZ HARIS JOHNSON.

It was by his middle name, Haris, that he became known to her mother and amongst their friends.

But Aayiz was the name in Aubrey's heart and the one she whispered when she cradled him close.

It meant replacement.

A gift.

In return for something lost.

Aubrey had felt as if she had lost her heart, and then her son had been born and she had found a piece of it again.

He was so beautiful.

So beautiful that when Aubrey first held him, in her slight haze, Aubrey panicked that surely they could tell just by looking who his father was, though her mom and aunt just readily accepted that Aubrey had no idea.

Aayiz, or Haris as they called him, was simply one of their own.

He had almond-shaped eyes that looked straight to your soul and caramel skin like his father's. He was a serious baby, but at four months old the smile that lit up his face when he saw Aubrey melted her.

The birth had been hard. Not so much physically— her training and stamina had meant Aubrey had coped well—but he had been born ten weeks early and that had been frightening.

It had been deeply painful too, though mainly on an emotional level.

She had wanted Khalid beside her and to know again the safe way he had made her feel when he was by her side, the way she had felt so looked after when he had given her a place to rest.

Aubrey had been grateful for the physical pain for it had given her a chance to cry out. She hadn't since the day she had rowed with her mom.

Things were better there now.

The Johnsons were survivors, even if her mom had gone under for a while. After their row, her mom had quickly accepted that there was a grandchild on the way and that had motivated her to find work. At first, Stella had done some housekeeping at one of the very expensive hotels on the Strip and it had twisted Aubrey's heart to see her mom trying to be brave while terrified. Aunt Carmel had gone on the bus with her sister for the first few shifts, but soon she'd taken the BHX herself.

Now her mom was one of the supervisors there.

Money was still a huge issue. Almost as soon as Stella had found work, Aubrey had had to quit dance and trapeze. She'd found some reception work for a couple of months, but the pay had been irregular.

Still, she had exercised daily and had been determined that as soon as she was able she'd be back on the trapeze and kicking her legs in Fremont Street.

Yet for all the struggle, Aayiz was worth it.

'You're as handsome as your daddy,' Aubrey told him as she cuddled him on her bed, stroking his silky black hair. She had waited for his eyes to turn the same burnt copper as Khalid's, yet they remained resolutely china blue. Still, they had the same way of looking directly into your soul, Aubrey thought as she ran a finger over and over his beautifully arched eyebrow, lulling him to sleep.

Aubrey missed Khalid every minute of every single day, and every minute of every single night. So badly she wanted to tell him about their son, but she just did not know how he'd react. And she could not get away from thinking of him for, like Khalid's pasta primavera, suddenly Al-Zahan seemed to be being mentioned everywhere.

A few nights ago, she had sat watching television and there had been a mention of the memorial being held for the anniversary of Jobe's death. Aubrey had tried to go but had been unable to afford it. She was still taking violin lessons but to get a discount had had to pay for ten weeks up front. Then breastfeeding hadn't worked, which had been another expense she hadn't been counting on.

At the mention of Jobe, she'd looked over at her

mom and seen the wistful look on her tired, scarred face, and had been so glad she hadn't been cruel on that difficult night when they'd rowed. Perhaps her mom had deep down known that she and Jobe would never be, but at least the dream of them had given her mom an escape.

Then the newsreader had spoken of the Devereux brothers' new venture, a grand hotel that was opening soon in Al-Zahan, and Aubrey had flushed as Khalid's face had appeared on the screen.

He wore a white robe and checked *kafeyah*, and that brief glimpse of Khalid had her heart leaping into her throat. He had a dark beard and looked so imposing, and so far from the man who had walked and held hands with her in Central Park. Aubrey's throat had closed tight as she'd waited for her mom to recognise him. To see that the son Aubrey held in her arms was the tiny image of him.

Yes, there were reminders of Khalid and his country everywhere.

Some of her friends were heading to Al-Zahan to earn tax-free dollars for the grand opening taking place in a couple of weeks. And just yesterday, when she'd flicked on the television, she'd landed on some Middle Eastern news channel and the image of a huge rose-gold palace, the cameras zooming in on the shimmering dome. She'd read the captions and seen that it was the palace in Al-Zahan.

She looked down at a now sleeping Aayiz and simply did not know what to do. Aubrey had never known who her own father was and she didn't want the same for her son.

A soft knock at the bedroom door told Aubrey that it wasn't her mom. She put a finger to her lips as Aunt Carmel came in. 'He's asleep,' Aubrey said.

'Can I hold him?' her aunt asked, and held out her arms. Her family and friends all doted on Aayiz, and soon Aunt Carmel was sitting on the bed, cradling her great-nephew. 'How are you doing?' she asked.

'Good,' Aubrey said.

'You're back on the trapeze.'

Aubrey nodded. 'Only in practice, and I've been doing some lyra routines.'

She had been waiting tables for a couple of months while training to get back to her regular work. Now she was in the air again and her body was finally starting to obey instructions, though she was taking it gently and wasn't quite ready to perform. 'I think I'm nearly ready to go back,' Aubrey explained, 'but I want to be sure. I've still got a couple of pounds to lose and I don't want to give Vince a reason to send me home again.'

'I'm asking because I ran into Brandy the other day. You know her, she was at Jobe's funeral. She was married to him, you know...'

'I know.' Aubrey smiled. Her mom and Carmel had told her that a thousand times since she'd returned with all the funeral details.

Well, not quite *all* the details!

'We used to call her Randy Brandy,' Carmel mused. 'She runs a dance school now.'

Aubrey nodded. She knew that too.

'Brandy needs to find some performing artists to send to Al-Zahan for the grand opening. They're flying a representative in for the auditions but all her girls that are good enough have already signed up. They need a few more and Brandy wants the commission. She asked about you.'

Aubrey stopped nodding.

'It's really good money,' Carmel added.

'I'm not ready to perform.'

'You just said you almost were, anyway. It's only background stuff, nothing you can't handle. You should at least have a word with Brandy, she gave me her card,' Carmel said, and placed it by the bed.

'I'm not leaving my baby, he's only four months old.'

'You were talking about going to Jobe's memorial service,' Aunt Carmel said.

'But I didn't,' Aubrey pointed out. 'Anyway, I'd have only been away for one or two nights.'

'It's for one week and one show and it's business class flights all the way,' Aunt Carmel said. 'With the money you make you might be able to pull back on those extra shifts. It would mean more time spent with Haris in the end.'

'It's not happening.'

'Give it some thought,' Aunt Carmel suggested, and she put the little baby down in the Moses basket that Aubrey's friends had given her when he was born.

He would soon be too big for it and she would have to buy a cot. She also needed a pram as he was getting too heavy for her mom to carry when Aubrey worked.

But her decision had little to do with money.

If she went to Al-Zahan, it might mean seeing Khalid. She was desperate to see him, but...

She had waited and waited for her feelings to fade, yet they hadn't.

She opened her bedside table and took out the silver bottle that she kept hidden in a sock and inhaled again his scent, recalling a time when she'd first turned around and seen him.

When Khalid had stood close and the night between them hadn't yet occurred.

She wouldn't change it, even if she could, Aubrey knew, looking over at Aayiz and hearing the little sleeping noises he made, and she wondered again about telling Khalid.

Could this be her one chance to?

Almost instantly she dismissed it. The opening night was going to be huge. Even if Khalid was there, he'd hardly notice her in costume amongst the many, many performers.

Yet he might.

There was the slimmest chance of seeing him again and Aubrey did not know how to resist.

And even if she didn't, at least she'd be able to see for herself the rose-pink palace and someday tell Aayiz about his daddy's country, having seen it first-hand. Aubrey would never risk taking Aayiz there, but this way, when he asked one day, at least she could tell him about the land his daddy was from.

She missed Khalid so very much.

So much that she was actually considering leaving her son, not just for money, or to find out more about his heritage, more for the chance of one distant glimpse of Khalid.

No, those feelings hadn't faded, for she craved him still.

As her mom and Aunt Carmel chatted outside, Aubrey took out the card and called Brandy and an audition was duly arranged.

CHAPTER ELEVEN

AL-ZAHAN WAS BEYOND her wildest dreams.

Aubrey could not believe that she was here in Khalid's kingdom.

Leaving Aayiz had been hard, but her mom had been wonderful about taking care of him. 'Carmel and I will not let him out of our sight,' she had said as Aubrey stood with her case about to head for the shuttle bus to the airport. Her mom had been holding him on her knee and pulling faces and making the serious little boy giggle.

Aayiz had done wonders for her mom. He didn't care about her burns—he looked at Stella without wincing and smiled at her scarred face, especially when she pulled funny faces, which she was doing now. 'There's something by the television for you, Aubrey.'

'I'm all packed...' Aubrey started, but then saw that there was a long slim package, wrapped in bright paper, and Aunt Carmel and her mom had smiled as Aubrey had opened it and promptly burst into tears.

It was a silver locket and inside there was a picture of Aayiz, and his huge blue eyes were as clear as if she were looking right at him.

'I'll never take it off,' Aubrey said.

'I thought as much.' Mom smiled. 'That's why we got a choker chain—you can wear it when you perform.'

Aubrey had broken down again as she'd thanked her aunt and mom, for she knew that a gift like this wouldn't have been easy for them to afford.

It was around her neck now, the locket resting in the hollow of her throat, and she felt as if Aayiz were here in Al-Zahan with her.

The staff complex was very luxurious. She had a vast suite overlooking the Al-Zahan desert. And though the rehearsals were long and intense, at the end of each day she was rewarded with long luxurious baths and deep-tissue massage.

Aubrey felt as if her body was finally her own again as it started to perform at its peak.

This morning the troupe had rehearsed in the foyer, but now final safety checks were being made. Sandbags were in place of people on the hoists and swings and a final lighting and sound-check was taking place.

Philippe, the choreographer, had recommended they all rest, but on the way back to the staff complex Aubrey had suggested that they scrap that idea and spend their one afternoon off sightseeing instead.

Aubrey was very aware that she might never be

able to bring Aayiz here, so she took a thousand photos on her phone. But she also put her phone away and tried to imprint Al-Zahan on her mind, the riot of sights, sounds and smells, so that she could one day tell him about the beauty of his father's land. How the buildings blended with the desert, how the rose-gold dome of the palace glittered in the afternoon sun. How ancient and modern married, for in the city skyline huge rose-gold towers stretched to the sky and tallest of all was the hotel that looked like a huge golden wave rolling in from the ocean behind.

It was an incredible feat of engineering, and Aubrey knew that Khalid would have had a lot of input into the design, and that made her feel so proud.

Tonight, after sunset, all the lights would be switched on, and there would be a light show before the chosen guests were invited to come inside the Royal Al-Zahan Hotel.

Aubrey loved Al-Zahan so much, and, though desperate to get home to Aayiz, there was a huge part of her that dreaded tomorrow coming, when she must leave.

Just a street away from the souks there were designer shops. Yet it was the souks that the troupe were to explore.

Their guide was incredible and took them from stall to stall, where they were offered samples of treats, like *harissah*, which sounded so like Aayiz's middle name that Aubrey was determined to like it before she had even tasted it. When she bit into the most delicious sweet coconut cake, she decided there and then that this would be the cake she would make for his first birthday.

And there were dates and nuts too, and little balls of dough with a filling that Aubrey had wanted to ask the name of, except they were being moved on down the busy street.

Gorgeous robes fluttered in the breeze in every colour, and Aubrey would have loved to buy one for herself, but, always mindful of money, she got Aayiz a trinket box instead, so that she could fill it with the little things she had collected while here.

And then they turned a corner and saw a crowd was gathered, taking in the stunning view of the palace with the ocean behind. The troupe joined them and enjoyed the sheer beauty of it all.

It killed her to think Khalid might be in there this very minute. To be so close and for him not to know that she was near.

Would he even want to know?

A year apart had blurred things. Aubrey knew how she felt, for barely a minute, let alone an hour, passed when she wasn't missing him. But the absolute clarity that she had belonged in his arms had faded, and now she wondered if Khalid had merely been saying the things she had wanted to hear at the time.

Sometimes Aubrey even wondered if she was turning into her mother and just living on dreams.

As she took a photo of the palace, the tour guide spoke.

'People gather here, for it is the best view of the main dome. We wait for the door on the east side to open and the goldsmith and mystic to come out. Then the bride will be chosen.'

Her heart stilled as she thought of the goldsmith Khalid had mentioned, but hadn't thought to question at the time. Aubrey thought too of the news bulletin she had seen, with the camera trained on the palace.

'An announcement is said to be imminent,' the guide said. 'Though that has been said for more than a year. But recently some activity in the palace has been seen. We expect it any minute now. Perhaps we will be lucky and they will come out and there will be a royal wedding...'

Oh, that would be so far from lucky, Aubrey thought, for she would surely die if she witnessed that.

'How soon after they come out is the wedding?' one of her troupe asked.

'If both the goldsmith and mystic come out then the wedding must take place within two sunsets. It has to be,' he said, 'or the country will fall.'

'Fall?' Aubrey frowned. 'Is that a myth?'

'No, it is not just a myth, it is written in ancient laws that if a wedding doesn't take place in the set time then our royal family will be disbanded and we will be ruled by the mainland. When the door opens, the clock starts ticking...'

So that was what Hussain had meant about the mainland rule, Aubrey realised.

One of the dancers asked a question. 'How does he choose his bride?'

'The Prince does not choose,' the guide answered. 'He has no part in the decision.'

'Why?'

'Because a young prince might think with his heart, when he must always be thinking what is best for his country. That is why the decision is left to the elders and ultimately the King.'

Aubrey had known that, but hearing it stated so factually she knew then there was no chance for them...

None at all.

Soon, Aubrey's little troupe were driven back to the staff quarters of the Royal Al-Zahan Hotel where they rested before the opening tonight, when Aubrey was hoping and praying that she would get a glimpse of Khalid.

Oh, but she wanted more than a glimpse.

Aubrey wasn't the only one who wanted to see the royals. The whole of Al-Zahan lined the streets and crammed into lookouts for a glimpse as a procession of cars drove from the palace.

The King went at the front, of course.

Behind him were Sheikh Princes Hussain and Abbad, and Sheikha Princess Nadia. Their rare appearance delighted the crowds.

But it was Sheikh Prince Khalid, with royal guests

the Queen and her husband the Prince Consort from the mainland, who were the recipients of the loudest cheer.

Khalid wore a black robe and silver *kefeyah*. On his shoulder was a whip and low on his waist was a tanned leather belt that held his *jambiya*—the jewelled handle of his dagger did not render it for display only. When he climbed out of the car, the mainland royals were introduced to the Devereux brothers and their wives.

'Abe and Naomi Devereux,' Khalid said. He had not expected Naomi to be here, given that she was due to give birth in a couple of weeks. Still, it broke the ice, for the Queen was expecting too.

'I am thrilled to be here for the opening.' The Queen smiled at Naomi.'

'And this is Ethan and Merida Devereux,' Khalid introduced, but the Queen really only had eyes for their daughter Ava.

'You must be so proud of your father,' the Queen crooned, and Khalid blinked.

Baby talk was an enigma to him.

The Queen craned her neck and looked upwards. 'It's an amazing feat.'

'It's a stunning piece of architecture,' Ethan politely agreed.

But the Queen smiled her Mona Lisa smile and only Khalid really knew what it meant.

The real feat was that the hotel had been built despite the objections of a cantankerous King.

'Finally,' Ethan said, as they stood awaiting the speeches and, ultimately, for the lights to be switched on.

'Indeed,' Khalid agreed, for it had been years in the planning.

Yet, despite the sense of achievement, despite the jubilation in the crowd, Khalid wanted the formalities to be over and for the lights to all be switched on in the Royal Al-Zahan Hotel. The speeches seemed to stretch for ever. He simply wanted it all to be over for he knew that Aubrey was inside.

Dressed in a gold leotard, she made her way through the back corridors and long internal stairwells of the grand hotel to assume her place.

Aubrey was part of the golden shimmer of a setting sun and though she knew she was just a small spoke in a very big wheel she was excited about performing tonight.

The extra sleep, the pampering, the amazing training facilities and balanced food had worked like an eraser on those last stubborn pounds and cobwebs of fatigue.

The foyer was vast, with an internal dome that at all times mirrored the current Al-Zahan sky. She had rehearsed in it all week, and at times felt as if she had flown in the dazzling blue sky. One afternoon, when the city had been drenched by a storm, it had felt as if she was dancing in the rain. Beautiful rain, though, for she remained dry and the sounds of the fountains muted the harsh elements outside.

Now, on a sultry desert night, Aubrey took the position on her hoop, which was suspended by invisible wires in the celestial night sky and bathed in stars, and she felt that if she reached out, she might touch one of the clouds drifting by.

She waited for her glimpse of Khalid, trying to tell her heart that a glimpse would suffice.

Though perched high in the atrium, Aubrey had a poor vantage point, for the clever design meant she couldn't see when the lights went on outside.

But she curled up in her hoop and touched her locket and felt that her baby's father was close.

The staff lined the entrance, and there was great anticipation as the orchestra started up and finally the moment was here and the grand entrance doors opened.

'Oh, Khalid,' Nadia breathed as she stepped in with her brothers. 'It is like stepping into paradise.'

The fountains, the graceful dancers in the sky, the gentle night breeze, it actually felt as if you stood in the desert on a magical night.

'Look,' Hussain breathed as he looked up and saw the night sky come slowly to life. Birds and warriors were stretching and waking. 'I thought they were statues…'

Khalid looked ahead, rather than up, for he refused to falter at this late stage. Tonight must be seamless. The King stood, bored, the Queen and Prince Consort were entranced. Khalid spoke with the wise elders who had entrusted him with this project and he was relieved by their clear approval, for their opinions were important to Khalid.

Yet even as duty prevailed he could feel the summons of Aubrey's eyes.

Look at me, look at me, she silently pleaded, curled up in a golden ball and looking down at Khalid.

He did not.

Even when the birds flew away and the warriors returned to their fires and her moment appeared as the sun set on a desert day, still she could not draw his gaze.

With grace and agility, up high, she moved into a slow handstand and the hoop slowly twirled, and she did not look down, lest she fall from the sky, yet she danced for him and she moved for him, and prayed that he could see.

He dared not.

'Your Highness…' Laisha murmured, for it was time to be on their way. The performance had concluded for now, and the schedule stated that they move to the elevators and to the top-floor restaurant where there would be fine dining, which Nadia was most looking forward to.

Instead there was a change of plan and Laisha murmured in his ear, 'The King is returning to the palace now.'

Khalid's jaw would once have gritted at the King's rude snub, but he had expected no less and dealt with it well.

'We shall move to the entrance and see him off,' Khalid said, when his darkest wish was that he would quietly disappear.

For ever.

Still, it was a relief when he was not around and the mood at the top table a little later was far more relaxed than it would have been with the King present.

'Tell me, Prince Khalid,' the mainland Queen said after the toasts, 'what is your next project?'

'We have more hotels in the pipeline.'

'I know that.' The Queen smiled. 'Tell me something I don't know.'

He must not, for Khalid had not even broached his vision with the King, so he made polite conversation instead.

His food was exquisite, of course it was, but for Khalid, a meal had not tasted as it should for more than a year. And while there was halva ice cream, at Khalid's request, surely it should not be tasted without Aubrey by his side?

Naomi and Abe were quiet throughout the meal, but still the Queen tried to draw Khalid out.

'Will you enjoy,' she asked as they dined, 'attending this type of event with your wife, to have someone by your side?'

No.

For his heart belonged elsewhere.

Instead of the truth he murmured a suitable reply and instantly regretted it, for the Queen, who was trying, blinked as if she had been snubbed.

'Prince Khalid,' Nadia said, for they spoke formally here, 'our late Queen would be so happy tonight.'

Indeed, Dalila would have been, for all her children were together, and the building of the hotel had gone ahead, despite the disapproval of the King.

'She would be,' Khalid agreed. He looked at Hussain, who looked anxious tonight, as he always did at formal events. And he looked at Abbad, who at fifteen now reminded Khalid of himself at the same age when he had first arrived in New York City and his lighter self had started to emerge.

Nadia troubled him, for her spirit was wild and he wished, how he wished, he knew how to address that, how to speak to her, how to warn her about boys, for they were taking an interest in her, and Nadia was returning it.

He wished he knew what to say to her and he knew that Aubrey would.

Aubrey.

She danced in his head, she spun in his head, as she had on the hoop in the foyer below, yet she was just as out of reach.

He had achieved so much, Khalid knew.

Not just the hotel, that was loose change compared to freedom for his siblings. He was bringing more joy and prosperity for his people, yet all at great cost to himself. For he could not waver from the path that his father dictated, or the sword would fall on Hussain and it would crush his brother.

Yet Khalid was no martyr.

He also yearned to be King and to completely rule this beautiful land.

It clawed at his throat, though, that for now he had to comply and hold back from ruling Al-Zahan as he saw fit, and making strong and deep relations with the mainland. And, worse, now that the hotel had been built, the excuses had ended and it was time now to accept the King's choice of a suitable wife.

There was no solution that worked for everyone.

At least, though, there would be a rare reprieve tonight.

'Five minutes, angels…'

Aubrey wriggled into the flimsy white costume with inbuilt knickers that she was to wear for the finale. The bodice was jewelled and the rest was sheer. She wore white trapeze boots, that were just slips of leather, and, having dressed, Aubrey frantically retouched her sparkly make-up as her hair was done.

With seconds to spare she held her locket between finger and thumb as she ran up the internal stairwells and through the back corridors, with burly guards pointing the backstage way.

As the esteemed guests left the celebrations and walked through the foyer, overhead would be a sleepy, angelic sky to wave them on their way.

And Aubrey knew it would be the last time she ever saw Khalid.

'Angels, take your places.'

She chalked her feet and hands and then climbed a long ladder and took to the platform and her hoop, and when she gave the signal she was ready she was lifted high into the dome.

She felt very safe with the equipment and had trained hard. The nerves fluttering in her chest were reserved for Khalid.

Aubrey knew now that she wasn't here for the extra money, or to find out about Aayiz's heritage. She was here for a far more pathetic reason—the mere chance to lock eyes with Khalid. To somehow let him know that he had been, and always would be, in her heart and in her thoughts, even if they could never be together.

The music was subtle, for it was not a show as such, more a pleasing feature as the dignitaries passed, but it thrummed through her as beautiful music should.

Aubrey felt teary at the strains of violin and the throb of bass and she took her gazelle position in the hoop, her head hanging downward, her left leg held straight while she held onto her right calf.

And she held her position, even while watching the beauty of him walking by.

Yet he did not see her.

She pulled herself up and sat in the hoop and waited the necessary beats until she performed the next move, for it was the doves' turn.

Now Khalid looked up.

And, when he did, Aubrey thought she might fly.

His eyes did not scan the foyer, he did not search for her amongst many, or try to pick her out, he just raised his noble head and looked straight into her eyes. And had he held out his arms she would have surely dropped into them for the pull of Khalid was so strong.

There was no question that he recognised her.

Her heart was sure of that, and she would hold onto this moment for ever, Aubrey knew.

This long moment when they locked eyes and the music felt like the score had been written for them, for the violin sounded as if it was crying.

She could not look away.

Even when Philippe scolded her for missing her next move, she would smile secretly to herself, for Khalid had seen her. The miles she had travelled, the separation from Aayiz was all worth it for this.

Until he withdrew his gaze.

Khalid looked away and turned to walk out and Aubrey realised that that brief moment was all she would have of him as, from on high, she was forced to watch him leave.

And a glimpse was no longer enough.

This whole week, and all the hope she had pinned on tonight, all the dreams she had suppressed in anticipation of this moment, ended in the most terrible anti-climax. She wanted to call out his name, to scream *Khalid!*, to tell him she loved him, if he would only turn around.

But he didn't.

Without even a backward glance he departed.

Aubrey couldn't even cry, for the show must go on and she was being paid very well after all.

And so she twirled and she stretched and she spun in the air for what felt like for ever, until finally the last of the esteemed guests had left and she could step down.

As she climbed down the ladder the only relief was that soon she could call home and check on Aayiz. But for now there was no chance to gather her breath, or to wipe the tears that were starting to fall. 'This way!' She was being directed up and Aubrey followed to where the stagehand was pointing.

And then up again, when Aubrey was sure she should be now heading down but the rest of her troupe weren't behind her.

Instead, two suited men were climbing the stairs but as she moved to flatten herself and let them pass they took her by the elbows.

'What are you doing?' Aubrey shouted, but they offered no response, just lifted her up so that her feet didn't touch the floor, carrying her, kicking and twisting, up the stairwell and then into a goods elevator, and then up, ever up, until she was taken, resisting, through an exit door and to a waiting helicopter.

And it was then that she knew that it was no accident or stroke of fate that had brought her here to Al-Zahan.

'Get off me,' she shouted, though of course to

no avail, for the wind from the rotors drowned her shouts, and the noise of them was deafening as they hurried her across the roof.

Aubrey wasn't scared of heights—she wouldn't be able to perform if that were the case—but the sudden ascent as the chopper lifted into the night sky had her stomach lurch and fear that she might simply disappear invade her.

Aayiz.

She wanted to scream his name as real terror took hold, as it dawned on her that if Khalid had arranged for her to be here, then he might already know about their son.

CHAPTER TWELVE

'WHERE ARE YOU taking me?' she demanded of the men, but then decided to save her strength.

Aubrey gave a wry laugh.

What strength?

She had no might against Khalid. She looked down on the vast desert, in trepidation rather than awe, and felt like nothing more than a speck, a tiny pawn in whatever game Khalid was playing.

They flew for what felt like for ever, though was probably closer to half an hour. There was no moon in the sky to orientate her, no markers she could see, until they hovered and the lights caught a huge white tent billowing in the desert winds. She could see horses fenced on one side, and at first they looked like toys, but they were soon low enough that Aubrey could see them startle and circle in alarm at the lights and noise.

And she was terrified but, as always, determined not to show it.

She was taken from the helicopter to a vast tented

complex. The air was cold in her lungs and the sky was a dense navy and she had never in her life seen more stars. There were universes swirling in a moonless sky and even the noise of the rotors was soon drowned by the shrieking winds.

Then silence as she stepped inside, only the silence wasn't soothing.

She was met by a woman but led by the guards along long white corridors towards the centre.

The air grew warmer and more scented, and Aubrey was in no doubt she was being led to him.

There was a fire pit in the centre and lavish drapes and rugs adorned the walls and there was a platform, but she could barely take in her surroundings, for there on the platform, more formidable, more powerful than she had ever known him, stood Khalid.

'You will kneel before the Sheikh Prince,' the woman said.

'I already knelt for him once and look where that got me,' Aubrey retorted, and she watched the tightening of his jaw.

'Kneel for the Sheikh Prince,' The woman urged.

'Not until I'm told why I'm here.'

'Leave her to me.' Khalid dismissed them and the woman and the burly men melted away so that she faced him alone.

'How have you been, Aubrey?'

'Fine, until I was kidnapped.' Her teeth were chattering but she was defiant.

'Don't be so dramatic,' he drawled. 'How else

was I to bring you here? This liaison has been most difficult to arrange.'

'Liaison?' Aubrey frowned.

'You surely don't think it was by accident that you are here in Al-Zahan.'

'Not now I don't,' Aubrey admitted, 'but for a while there I thought it was down to hard work.' Of all the things to cry about, and there were plenty, right now, that was the one that hurt the most.

She had been proud of being chosen, despite a less than brilliant audition.

Proud of the work she'd put in and the decent money she would finally earn.

Yet this was nothing more to him than a *liaison*.

Right now, she hated that word.

'How else was I supposed to get you here?' Khalid asked, bemused by the tears in her eyes, for he had been certain they would fall into each other's arms.

Instead she stood warily and looked at him with suspicious eyes.

'I hoped to see you at the memorial,' Khalid admitted, though he omitted to mention the gut-wrenching disappointment he had felt when she'd failed to arrive.

'I couldn't afford it,' Aubrey said in a hollow voice, not knowing how to tell him about their son. She looked at his narrowed eyes and knew he did not accept her pale excuse. Hell, if it hadn't been for Aayiz she'd have thumbed a lift for a chance of seeing him. 'How did you arrange it?' she asked, simply not getting it. 'My aunt was the one who told me about the auditions.'

'I spoke with Brandy at the memorial and from there Laisha arranged things.'

If the Sheikh Prince wanted a discreet liaison with a certain Vegas trapeze artist, then the Sheikh Prince got it.

And if the Sheikh Prince wanted said Trapeze artist to have no clue as to his hand in this, then of course that too could be arranged.

Except this was not the joyous reunion he had envisaged.

'Are you marrying soon?' Aubrey asked.

'I don't want to discuss that.'

'Neither do I,' Aubrey snarled, 'but it happens to be relevant, Khalid.'

He stepped down from the platform and as he approached he saw that Aubrey was shaking in fear, and he did not understand her terror.

'I am sorry if you had a fright, it was the only way to get you here...'

But it wasn't the method of her arrival that now terrified her.

It was that she was here and knew she must tell Khalid that he had a son.

She knew that she had to tell him. For more than a year her secret had been bursting inside her and now with only a wall of air between them, Aubrey did not know how to lie.

'We need to speak,' Aubrey said through chattering teeth.

'Later,' Khalid said. His hand came to her arm and she quaked at his touch and she could feel the locket on her throat jump with each nervous beat of her heart.

A year of no contact, a year of pain and lies, and she wanted to collapse in his arms and bury her head in his chest, but instead she trembled, in fear, in want and in anger, that he assumed she would simply succumb.

And in shame that she would.

'I meant,' Khalid rectified, 'first you need to eat.'

She shot out a hollow laugh. 'Eat?'

'You have been performing.'

She could not accept his friendliness, for she knew it might disappear when the truth was out.

'You need to eat,' Khalid pushed on. 'You are surely hungry.'

'Khalid...' She covered her eyes with her hands but there was no hiding there, yet the words simply would not come.

'It was a shock,' Khalid said, 'for you to be removed like that. I did not want to scare you but no one could know—'

'Khalid,' she broke in again, but it was hopeless, so her hands moved to her throat and she undid the clasp and handed the locket to him.

'What is this?'

'Open it.'

She almost dared not watch as he did, yet she forced

herself to, watching his long, deft, fingers deal with the tiny clasp, then she looked at his face.

Withheld was a word she had once used to describe him.

It felt apt now, for not by a flicker did Khalid give away what he was thinking.

Khalid did not know what to think.

Except for one thing—the baby was his.

To ask for clarification of that fact would be an entire waste of words. For he was there in the baby's features, and so too were his siblings and mother, yes, even his father the King.

There was no silence in the desert.

He could hear the flap of the tent walls and the shrieks from the wind. And he could hear the crackle of wood from the fire pit, yet he could not hear his heart.

Odd when he could feel the quickening beat of it as it pounded in his chest.

How could he not have known?

How, Khalid begged of himself, could he simply not have known that his child had been born?

'You never thought to tell me?'

Aubrey dragged in a breath when finally he spoke, but it did not steady her voice, for it came out high and strained. 'I've thought of telling you every day.'

'Yet you didn't,' Khalid said. 'Had I not brought you here, were you ever going to tell me you had given birth to my child?'

'I don't know,' Aubrey admitted.

'What sort of answer is that?'

'An honest one.'

'How can a liar claim to be honest?'

She wished he would roar, for the icy calm of his voice was more terrifying. She wanted to flee but there was nowhere to run and nowhere to hide so she faced him.

'You told me it would be unprecedented.' Aubrey was the one who was shouting. 'You warned me that I could not get pregnant by you…'

'But you did?'

'Yes, I did,' Aubrey said, and all the terror of these months rose within her then, all the anger she had held onto was unleashed and she pummelled at his chest. 'And I dealt with it, because I was scared how you might…'

'Might?' He caught her wrists. 'Meaning?'

'That you'd make me get rid of my baby.'

'No.'

'Or that you'd bring him here where I couldn't be with him.'

'Him?'

'Him.' She nodded, and the tears she cried then were not for herself but for Khalid, for he hadn't even known he had a son. 'Aayiz. Our son is called Aayiz.'

'Replacement.' Khalid's voice was husky. 'For something lost.'

'Except he could not replace you. I love him so much but he cannot replace you…'

'Then you should have told me!' His voice was rising, the truth taking hold. He was aware that this news could bring him down, for his father would like nothing more than to dispose of the next in line, and move a more malleable Hussain into place. But that was not what troubled him now. 'I should have been informed.'

'How?' she demanded. 'Should I have left a message with the palace switchboard? Or gone to newspapers perhaps? You didn't give me contact details…'

Deliberately so, for it would have been beyond impossible to resist.

He had been coming to thin air for more than a year, his body screaming for her, and the only barrier had been distance and that he would have to call in others to be with her again.

Even then he had given in.

She was, after all, here.

'Aayiz Haris Johnson.' She watched his eyes briefly shutter when she gave Aayiz's surname. 'He was born ten weeks early.' And she watched his face pale. 'He did so well, Khalid,' Aubrey told him. 'He only needed a little bit of oxygen and help with his feeds.'

He could have died and Khalid would not have even known of his existence. 'You should have told me!' he roared.

For the first time this contained man shouted and his anger was returned straight back to him tenfold.

'And what if I had?' Aubrey shrilled. 'What would have been your *solution*, Prince Khalid?' She was angry on behalf of them, rather than at him, but she let Khalid have it anyway, goading him with her words. 'You can please your people, you can take the strain from Hussain, and you can please your father, but that doesn't solve us! There is no solution, Khalid.'

He *loathed* the burden, the constraints on his life. In that moment he loathed it so much that on a whim he tore off the *kurbash* he wore on his shoulder, unsheathing the *jambiya* in one deft motion, to discard it, but it terrified Aubrey and she screamed.

'Aubrey!' He did not shout now, his voice was clear and measured. 'I removed them so as not to intimidate you.'

She looked at him then and the scary desert warrior she had somehow been confronted by simply faded and before her stood the man she knew. 'Khalid, I didn't know what to do.'

Neither did he but now he could hear his heart, now it roared in his ears and it flooded his veins.

Love was a luxury denied to him, yet here it stood in front of him, and it was not just the thought of something happening to Aayiz that terrified him but all that might have happened to her.

He was through with niceties and accepting her independent ways.

He wanted his forbidden family here.

Here in Al-Zahan where he could keep them protected and safe.

Here.

'Khalid?'

He heard her voice, and saw her wide eyes. She was breathing hard as if she'd been running, and he could see the pointed nipples rise and fall on her chest. Her breasts were a little bigger, but that was the only physical difference he could see.

He wanted to be witness to every inch of her, though.

Khalid wanted her again as his.

With his look Aubrey felt the summons of his desire roll through her.

She felt her own pulse in her neck match the throb between her thighs, and a lick of want curled her insides, though she fought to remind herself that they needed to speak.

Fought to convince herself that she did not need his touch, and that she could deny his kiss.

Yet *now*, when he held out his arms, she flew into them with as much force as if she'd fallen from her hoop in the sky.

A year of pain and of loss didn't fade as they touched; instead, it ratcheted up as his mouth again reclaimed hers.

He knew now.

And there were no words that could help for neither knew the answers; touch sufficed for now.

Almost.

The thoughtful lover she had known was gone on this dark desert night. He was bearded and rough with his kisses and his tongue forced her mouth open and allowed for no breath.

The force of him toppled her backwards but his arms cushioned her landing.

He slid the belt from his robe and tore at her flimsy costume, exposing her breasts, and then he ripped at the little enclosed panties.

'Forgive me,' he said as his thighs roughly parted her legs.

'Nothing to forgive,' she moaned between hot kisses.

Yet it was Khalid who remembered. 'Will it hurt after the baby?'

'I don't know,' she admitted, though she was frantic to find out, and she moaned as he slowly entered and she stretched as he filled her. The shudder he gave told of Khalid's gratification to be inside her at last. 'No,' she said, for it did not hurt.

A year of suffering was removed.

He rose up on his arms and he placed them either side of her head and he looked right into Aubrey's eyes.

She touched his face, she touched his shoulders, she felt his power ignite her again, even when weak in his arms.

Aubrey felt the tiny warnings from her body, and he drove harder and faster, and then he stilled and shot power the length of her spine. Yet even as she came she sobbed, for he pulled out. 'Khalid…'

It was unexpected, delicious, empty, as he pulsed over her, and Aubrey eased up on her elbows, watching as he stroked the last drops onto her. She was breathless and satisfied, yet not. 'I'm on the Pill.'

'So you said.' His words came out dark and accusing, but he was holding onto the edge for dear life, for it had taken more willpower than Khalid had thought he possessed to pull out.

She went to get up, to huff in offence, but he pulled her back into his arms and would not let her walk off. 'I want to take care of you both...' He hesitated.

'But...?' Aubrey asked, for she knew that there was one.

Khalid offered no response.

CHAPTER THIRTEEN

'BUT...?' SHE VENTURED AGAIN.

Instead of answering, Khalid suggested that she eat and then they would speak.

And while she would far rather lie in his arms, the simple fact was that she was hungry.

There was another reason, though.

Aubrey wanted a table between them while they discussed *their* son. She did not want the balm of his arms, for she wanted to pay full attention.

Aayiz came first, last and always. He had since the night she had found out that she was expecting him, and nothing was going to change that. She didn't know what Khalid would suggest, or how much visitation he might want, but she was grateful for the chance to eat and to regroup.

He showed her where she could freshen up and told her that food would soon be served.

Aubrey parted a drape and stepped into an area lit by pretty lanterns. It seemed odd that in the middle of the desert there was a warm bath already drawn.

There was no #71 to dial here, for it was all taken care of.

Aubrey swirled her hand in the milky water. The scent was floral yet not sickly sweet and her skin was soft and oily when she removed her hand and she just could not resist climbing in.

The sigh she gave was not just because of the bliss of the water on her tired, aching muscles but more that Khalid finally knew about Aayiz.

It felt as if a huge burden had been lifted.

Aubrey rinsed off and then climbed out of the deep bath. The oils formed little drops on her body and there were no towels that she could see, and so Aubrey massaged the oil into her skin and looked around for something to cover her.

There were no bath robes either and she padded through to a draped area that looked like a dressing room, for there were mirrors and jewels, silk scarves and perfumes too.

There was also a crimson velvet robe on a stand with a jewelled collar and huge jewelled cuffs.

He really had planned this, Aubrey realised, imagining his aides preparing the tent, and that unnerved her all over again.

Even with her bombshell, it still felt as if Khalid was ahead.

She lifted the robe and though the velvet was soft and warm between her fingers and she was starting to shiver, Aubrey left it on the stand.

She was sick and tired of dressing for men.

It didn't take long to find a pale muslin slip that was probably an undergarment, but it felt a whole lot better than crimson velvet. Then, having run a comb through her hair, she ignored the glass bottles and potions and instead placed a heavy silk fringed scarf around her shoulders before heading out.

Khalid made no comment as she took a seat at the low table.

He dared not.

For, if he did, he might tell her that she reminded him of the day they had met, when she had held a scarf around her shoulders.

And he might tell her that she reminded him of that first night when he had come to her room and seen her pale, fragile features without make-up, or that day in the park when he had first realised his deep love. But that would be cruel.

For if love could fix this then it already would have.

'You're not eating,' Aubrey said, when she saw there was only a place set for one.

'I ate at the hotel,' Khalid said. 'I had this prepared for you.'

'What is it?' Aubrey asked, because the aromas were amazing as she lifted a lid on a small earthenware pot in front of her.

'Piti,' Khalid said. 'Lamb and chickpeas…'

There was saffron and mint in it too, Aubrey thought as she took her first taste. It was completely delicious.

'It translates to "soup for the soul".'

'The translation is correct.' Aubrey smiled.

There was *qutab* too, a bready pancake stuffed with cheese and lamb. And as she bit in to it, she was very grateful that he did not push her for answers, for she was indeed seriously hungry.

'There was a staff party after the performance,' Aubrey explained. 'With lots of food and things.'

'Are you sorry you missed it?'

'No,' Aubrey admitted. 'I'm just saying I would have eaten by now. This is nice.'

'Good.'

There was black tea with cubes of sugar and lemon, served in heavy crystal glasses, and it was refreshing and sweet all at once.

He watched as colour warmed her cheeks and he held back from saying what he had to, unsure how it would be received, and wanting her to have had nourishment first, so instead of asking about Aayiz he asked about her instead.

And always she surprised him.

'I've been having violin lessons.'

'For how long?'

'Since…' She thought back. 'Since a couple of weeks after we met. Nobody knows,' she added.

'Why not?'

Aubrey took a mouthful of *piti* before answering him. Khalid was right, it really was food for the soul, for it was warming and nourishing and it gave her a pause to think before answering. Why hadn't she told her aunt and mom? 'I feel a little bit guilty, I guess,' Aubrey admitted. 'I wasn't working for a while...'

'You supported your mother when she didn't.'

'I know,' Aubrey agreed. 'And that's why I chose to stay quiet.' She gave him a smile. 'I love my mom. I do. I absolutely do, but she sure knows how to push my buttons.'

Khalid smiled, and as he did so it occurred to him he had barely smiled for a year, yet the very curve of her lips had him doing the same.

'And,' Aubrey continued, 'I knew if I told her then she'd think of a million things I should be doing instead with my time and money.' She liked it that Khalid said nothing, that he waited for her to think and then to elaborate. 'I need my music, Khalid. I need something that is just for me.'

'I agree.'

'What do you have that is just for you?' she asked, tearing a piece of *qutab* and giving him half.

Without thinking, Khalid took it and dipped the bread in her bowl.

No longer strangers, and closer to each other than he had ever imagined they could be.

'I don't have...' He was about to point out that he really didn't have time, yet that wasn't quite right. 'I draw.'

'You can draw?' Aubrey said. 'Wow!'

'No, there is no wow to my drawings,' Khalid said, 'they are technical ones.' He adored her slight frown. 'I picture Al-Zahan how to my eyes it should be.'

'Such as?'

Khalid swallowed, for his sketches were made here in the desert and then burnt, for his visions were not for others, yet he looked at Aubrey and he *wanted* to share them with her.

'I would like to see a sea bridge link us to the mainland.'

He waited for her to tell him how impossible that would be, or perhaps he wanted his own 'wow'. Instead, she shuddered.

'What?' Khalid asked.

'You'd never get me on one.'

'Says the woman who flies in the sky.'

'True,' Aubrey admitted, and then she thought of the stunning Royal Al-Zahan hotel, and all the genius in his very private mind. She would dance on any sea bridge he built! She would walk a tightrope to the mainland if it had been designed by those knowing eyes. 'It sounds amazing,' Aubrey said, and really thought about it. 'Wow.'

Khalid stayed silent, for even he could not comprehend just how much it helped to hear that from Aubrey.

'Have you done anything about it?' she asked.

'No,' Khalid said. 'The King considers the hotel to be an abomination. He loathes the mainland too...'

'Do you?'

'Not at all. Their Queen is a kind and wise ruler. I have made much effort to forge better relations but, of course, the king does his best to dismantle any progress made. Take tonight—he left after the speeches, and it was a snub.'

'Ah, but while the cat's away…'

Khalid frowned. 'The cat?'

'It's a saying. While the cat's away the mice will play.'

'I don't play games, Aubrey.'

'Perhaps you should…' Her hand went to creep across the table but she pulled it back. Aubrey had never flirted in her life, but it came readily to her when she was with him. She wanted to play, she wanted to demand halva ice cream for dessert.

She wanted, she wanted, she wanted.

But there were such important things that simply had to be discussed first.

And so she mopped the last of the *piti* and popped the last of the *qutab* into her mouth, and swallowed it down, and she looked at her empty plate and re-membered again how kind he had been in the over-whelming restaurant that night.

Oh, that night. 'I had an ear infection when I met you.'

'I remember.'

'I was taking some of my mother's antibiotics, but I didn't know they affected the Pill.'

'It doesn't matter now,' Khalid said.

'Believe me, it did at the time,' Aubrey said, and rolled her eyes, but then she was serious. 'I had no idea.'

'How did your mother take it?'

Aubrey stared at her empty plate and decided that there were some conversations that didn't need to be repeated. 'Not brilliantly at first, but she soon came round. She's been great actually.'

'And how have you been?'

'Well.'

'Aubrey?'

'I have been,' she insisted. 'He's such a wonderful baby, Khalid. He's serious like you, but when he smiles…' And she suddenly felt as if she was trying to sell her son to an unwilling buyer. 'He's so like you, I always tell him he's his father's son.'

'Aubrey,' Khalid said, and he reached for her hand. 'I know it has been a struggle, but those days are over now. You can live here with your child, and I shall see you when I can…'

'When you choose?' Aubrey checked, and he slowly nodded and even held her eyes as he spoke on.

'And you and Aayiz would live in luxury in a compound by the palace, and at times I would bring you here.'

'With our son?'

'No, I would bring you here to spend time with me.'

'And what would *our son* do?'

'He will not be recognised as my son.'

Aubrey thought she had known heartache.

In this difficult year, she thought she had known pain and loss.

Now she met its maker.

'I hate you for that, Khalid.'

'I know,' Khalid said, for he hated that of himself too. 'But it is the law and I am not yet King.' He breathed, and he looked at her furious eyes. 'But this way I could take care of you and the baby.'

'His name is Aayiz,' Aubrey said. 'He looks like you and he is serious like you and he smiles like you. How can you say he is not your son?'

'Aubrey, I told you from the start we cannot be and that you cannot get pregnant by me. I knew you could not accept the rules.'

'Well, I did get pregnant…' She choked on her sobs. 'And I was terrified, and I got ill, and I was even more scared, and when Aayiz was born two months early I have never been more petrified in my life, but he is my son, and so I dealt with it. And as I said to my mother, I *will* raise my son. If you really think I'm going to join your harem…'

'It would not be a harem. There would be only you.'

'Oh, that's right. I'd be your *ikbal*—your chosen one, your favourite one. Screw you, Khalid.'

'Don't be vulgar.'

'You tell me to be your whore and then you tell me not to be vulgar? You're quite a contradiction, Sheikh Prince Khalid.'

'Silence!' Khalid said. 'Listen. You can make your music for me.'

Aubrey laughed.

'I wasn't joking.'

'That's the part that made me laugh.' But not for long. Aubrey was serious now. 'I would live here and our son would have no status?'

'Who would want this status?' Khalid said. 'It would be better for him than carrying the weight of the crown. He would be educated, wealthy...'

'Still a bastard,' Aubrey said. 'And I'm allowed to say that about him, no one else,' she said, 'and I'm doubly allowed to say that, because I'm one too.' She looked at him.

'No.' Aubrey held strong, more for Aayiz than herself. 'You can do better.'

'This is not a negotiation,' Khalid said.

'This conversation is over then.'

She demanded better, insisted on better, and Khalid laid every card he had on the table. 'I will speak with the King.' And deal with the elders and the uproar from his people and the hungry press. But he did not burden her with that. 'Instead of here, you can live in America, and I will see you there.'

'And our son?' Aubrey checked.

He nodded. 'It would be less disrespectful to my wife if you are abroad.' The rules felt like hot coals that he juggled as he tried to do better by Aubrey than his father had by his mother.

'You'll be marrying then?' Aubrey checked.

'Of course.'

'And do I get to have a husband?'

'No.'

'Then this conversation really is over, Khalid.'

In her wildest imaginings, she had anticipated a battle of wills regarding their son, for him to demand to see him, to be furious at not being informed.

Not this cold indifference to their beautiful boy.

She was nothing, neither was her son. 'Over and over you hurt me, Khalid,'

'I would never hurt you.'

'But you do, you do, you do. Every time you tell me I'm not suitable, every time you tell me that we could never be. Well, no more.' Aubrey was tough—she'd had to be—and she faced him with clear, angry blue eyes. 'I don't need you, Khalid.' He opened his mouth to refute that but she spoke fast, lest she waver. 'I never knew my father and I survived.'

'Bare…'

He was about to say barely, about to point out what she had to do to survive, yet he looked at her, proud and strong, and there was no *barely* about it.

It was humbling to know that Aubrey and his child would survive without him. Not just that, he could see that Aubrey would thrive.

'You'll have other sons, Khalid. Ones deemed worthy to be royal and to be recognised. I won't let my son be second best.

'You cannot expect my son to be raised in a trailer park…'

'Khalid.' She stopped him right there. 'If I am to raise him singlehanded then I need my family and friends around me, and that's where they happen to be.'

'I shall give you enough money—'

'And that money will go towards his education, and when I consider him old enough, Aayiz will be a wealthy young man. He'll also know the value of hard work and he'll know the value too of a strong, independent woman.' That Khalid thought he could buy her angered Aubrey. 'I'm not a martyr, Khalid. If I can't make the rent then I'll dip into the funds, but I'll do my damnedest not to.'

'Does it abhor you to take money from me?'

'Yes.' Aubrey nodded. 'I won't be like my mother, Khalid. History won't repeat itself. I will not sit in some home, kept by you, waiting for the master to arrive.'

'You cannot see anyone else.'

'Oh, but I shall,' Aubrey said. They were laying down the rules and their love lived or died this night, so she told him how it would be. 'I want love in my life, Khalid, and I'm sure I'll find it. Someone nice, who loves my son as if he were his own.' Tears were streaming down her face now yet she was strong against this immutable man.

'And when Aayiz asks about his real daddy, I'll say he didn't want to know you. He sent us money, and I saved it for you for when you're older, Aayiz, but I raised you myself. And I'll make love to my husband and thank God for a man who loves me and my son…' She gave Khalid pain, for she saw it flicker across his face, before he composed himself and then refuted her bold, provocative words.

'You could never want another man as you want me.'

'Rubbish,' she both sneered and lied. She knew a few tricks, even if she'd never used them till now, but she had been taught how to make a man burn. 'I might touch myself to the memory of you every now and then…' she watched the tightening of his lips '…but it will be my husband who satisfies me.'

'Never.'

'For ever,' Aubrey clarified. 'You don't get it, do you? I want you. All of you. I want you as his full-time father, and I want your bed at night. And if I can't have that, then I sure as hell won't sit in the desert, waiting for my turn with the master.'

'Aubrey, I would marry you tomorrow if I could but I cannot move mountains until I am King.'

'Then call for the helicopter,' Aubrey said. 'I want to go home.'

'We cannot leave now—here is the only place we can speak freely. Why do you think I went to such lengths to bring you to the desert?'

'I want to go home,' Aubrey insisted.

'You *cannot* leave with nothing resolved.'

'Nothing can be resolved, Khalid,' Aubrey responded, 'until you're King. I won't be your mistress in the meantime. Now, please, I want to go home to *my* son.'

'Your Highness.' Laisha, who stood with an aide, was smiling as she met them in the VIP lounge. The helicopter ride had been a turbulent hell and now, as they came in from the rooftop, Aubrey stood in a hijab as his assistant approached with an aide, and she realised Khalid had been right to ask her to stay longer in the desert.

Yet she had insisted she wanted to go home.

Now!

There was no chance of them speaking, there would be no final words. Their goodbyes, Aubrey now realised, should have been said in the desert.

The Prince had been gone for twelve full hours and there was plenty Laisha had to brief him on. 'The opening went so well, the feedback has been amazing.'

Khalid wanted privacy. He wanted his royal suite and to convince Aubrey to stay, for it could not end like this.

Except there were demands on his time.

Always.

'Exciting news.' Laisha beamed. 'The first baby has been born on the hundredth floor.'

'Very good,' Khalid said, although her words were all white noise to him.

'Naomi Devereux had a little girl in the early hours. Abe has asked if you would call in.'

'I don't have time.'

'But, Your Highness, I rescheduled for you.'

'Very well,' Khalid snapped. 'Laisha, please give us a moment…'

Laisha and the aide reluctantly stepped aside, but it was hardly private, and Aubrey very deliberately did not look up at him.

They stood *almost* alone but it wasn't enough, and Khalid looked at her huge blue eyes and he could not bear to let her go. Had she demanded his money, his time, his passion, he could have dealt with them all.

But Aubrey insisted on his heart.

Each corner of it.

'Stay for a few days…'

'No.' She ached for Khalid, yet she ached for her baby, and her body was tired from last night, but most of all she was scared she would relent.

She wanted his desert bed.

And the balm of his kiss and to be made love to each night, and more of the beautiful dark babies they made.

And she wanted his strength and to be cared for.

No, it would be so dangerous to stay.

'Aubrey?'

'I can't, Khalid. I've already been away long enough.'

'Then at least think about what I have offered.'

'I've told you the answer's no,' Aubrey said, and now she looked at him. And of all the difficult things about this strange and beautiful land, the hardest was that she could not touch him now, or lean on him, or kiss him goodbye. She heard the cough of the aide, hurrying them along, and she could feel Laisha's nervousness, for they really should not be speaking alone.

They could not touch.

And yet he did.

She closed her eyes at his soft, forbidden kiss. She tried to pull away, yet her body refused to deny her this last moment of bliss.

He held her face as his mouth caressed hers and she was crying and shaking as his hand slid beneath the silk scarf and she felt his fingers soft on her neck.

And not by a flicker did she flinch as the silver chain around her neck broke.

'Trust me,' Khalid said.

'I want to.' Oh, so badly she wanted to trust a man. *This* man.

'Trust me,' he said again. 'I shall never stop striving to better us.'

And then, because he had to, he let her go.

Khalid watched as Aubrey left the sumptuous VIP room. He willed her to look back, to run back, but she did not.

A purple-faced Laisha forced a smile. 'Your Highness. Shall we make our way to the hundredth floor?'

The aide was grim and no doubt itching to get back and tell the King, but Khalid didn't care, for there was far more on his mind.

Of course he must visit Naomi and Abe and do the right thing, but worlds were colliding as he took the elevator to the hundredth floor.

'I can take it from here, thanks,' Khalid said, and he shot the aide a withering look as the man took a seat with Laisha in one of the waiting rooms and Khalid made his way to the luxurious suite.

A nurse was just leaving and Khalid realised he did not know how to smile as he walked in.

'Congratulations,' Khalid said, and shook hands with Abe.

'Thanks,' Abe said. 'I have to admit I was nervous when Naomi went into labour, but she couldn't have had better care. The facilities are amazing.'

'Excellent.' Khalid gave a tight smile.

But then he looked at Naomi who sat up in bed, and he smiled naturally, for how could he not? She was cradling her tiny baby, wrapped in the softest pink blanket and just *adoring* her newborn infant.

But then Khalid's smile wavered and he felt closer to tears than he had in fourteen years and the one time he had cried. He had never been jealous in his life before, and certainly not of the Devereuxes. They were friends, more like family. But seeing Abe take the infant from Naomi, seeing the mother elated, tired and yet cared for, gnawed at his gut, for who had been there for Aubrey?

Not him.

'Here,' Abe said, and deposited six tiny pounds of infant into his arms, and it was the heaviest load Khalid had ever held.

She was so little and light and smelled as Hussain had that long-ago day when his mother had introduced his new brother to him.

Khalid had seen Hussain even before the King had, and he'd looked at his baby brother and had vowed to protect him and keep him safe.

And he remembered holding the tiny, motherless twins, two days after they had arrived.

He had vowed the same to them.

Now Khalid's strong arms ached for Aayiz.

'What is her name?' Khalid asked, yet his voice came out all wrong, for it sounded as if he needed to clear his throat.

Which he did.

'Hannah,' Naomi said. 'It means favour or grace…'

I have a son, Khalid wanted to say.

But he did not.

Instead he said and did the right things, but all he could think of was Aubrey, and that she had been through all this alone. And those thoughts led to little Aayiz, who surely he should vow to protect and keep safe too.

Yet to do that required not just a mountain to be moved but the ravines and the sky too.

Out in the corridor he took out the locket he had taken from Aubrey and his heart seemed to rise to his throat while his breath hitched as he stared at *his* son.

His beautiful son, with black hair and caramel skin.

And not just his son, but hers too.

Aayiz had Aubrey's eyes.

And he wanted them here by his side.

'Khalid?' He was torn from his thoughts by a female voice, and for a second Khalid braced himself, expecting Laisha with more urgent appointments for him.

But it was the mainland Queen.

Alone.

She wore black linen pants and a loose white shirt, and looked relaxed and happy.

'Your Highness.' Khalid was confused but supremely polite. 'I trust all is well?'

'Of course, Khalid. I asked for a private tour and I have been shown around. The nurse said to have a wander.' She smiled. 'It is gorgeous, I wish we had such a facility. I just said to my husband I would love to have the baby here.'

'We would be proud if you chose to.'

'And what about the King?' the Queen said. 'I am speaking of your father's reaction if we had our child here, Khalid, not you.'

'Well, you would be made most welcome.' Though his heart was heavy he was actually glad of the chance to speak with the Queen. 'I would like to apologise if I seemed rude last night.'

'Of course not.' She smiled. 'It was a splendid night. I was too forward, enquiring about your future wife, when nothing has been announced.'

Always Khalid faced her at long tables, or with aides present, but despite the constraints and the feuds in their countries' histories, he had always found her quite charming.

Progressive.

When she had been crowned he had been pleased, and had always looked forward to the day they might work together for their respective people.

While the cat's away... He understood now what Aubrey had meant. In fact, it was as if she now stood next to him.

He looked towards the vast floor-to-ceiling windows and the glittering view of the Arabian Sea, and he took...not really a gamble, rather he pressed fast forward on a dream.

'You asked last night what my ideas for Al-Zahan were.'

'Indeed I did.' The Queen smiled. 'But please, Khalid, don't bore me with talk of hotels.'

'I shan't bore you.'

He held up his hand, entwined within it a silver chain, and he pointed to the horizon beyond.

And he told her what he saw in the future.

CHAPTER FOURTEEN

THE KING LAUGHED.

And Khalid had never once seen him do so.

He laughed and he laughed and then he stopped laughing and glared at his son who dared defy him and insisted on choosing his own bride.

'You are telling me that you want to marry a Vegas stripper and make her our Queen and that I am to approve it?'

'Aubrey is a dancer.'

'She is a stripper with a bastard child.'

'Her name is Aubrey,' Khalid said. 'And my son's name is Aayiz and they have my heart.'

'Well, we don't deal in hearts here,' the King said coldly. 'You have lost your mind, Khalid. What could this woman bring to Al-Zahan?'

'So much,' Khalid said. 'She is fierce and she is forgiving, and understands people's foibles yet does not judge, and she works harder than anyone I know.'

'Khalid, I am weary of your constant delay to your

duties. I am summoning the mystic and goldsmith and your bride shall be chosen by me.'

'I have already chosen my bride,' Khalid said.

'Then you relinquish your right to the throne and it shall fall to Hussain.'

Khalid stared at his father, saw his devious smile and loathed the man who would make Hussain's nightmare come true. It was no idle threat, for the King called for his vizier. 'In two sunsets there shall be a royal wedding. Bring me Sheikh Prince Hussain—'

'I shall marry,' Khalid said. 'Send the goldsmith and the mystic to the dome, and tell them a bride is being chosen for Crown Prince Khalid.'

He watched as the orders were given and as the door to the palace dome opened, cheers were let out across Al-Zahan, and it was announced that Crown Prince Khalid's bride would soon be chosen and a wedding would be taking place.

It was done.

But not quite, for again he looked at his father, who thought he had got his way, and Khalid addressed him in a deep and even tone. 'The saddest day of my mother's life was when she was chosen by you…'

'I made her Queen.'

'You never made her feel like one, though.'

He was calm and he was steady as at length he addressed the King. Only he did not pour oil on troubled waters.

Instead, Khalid lit the fuse.

* * *

Aunt Carmel and her mom were sitting on the porch when Aubrey returned from Al-Zahan. She managed a wide smile and they kindly did not mention her red swollen eyes.

'Haris might be awake,' her mom said, but before she dashed inside, Aubrey corrected her.

'Aayiz,' Aubrey said. 'He's to be called Aayiz from now on. Haris is his middle name.'

He wasn't awake, but still Aubrey scooped him up and his face lit up with a smile when he saw that his mommy was here.

'I love you, Aayiz,' she told him, and she cried hot, angry tears on him, and then they changed to sad ones too for she knew a truth, even if Khalid did not. 'Daddy loves you too. So, so much, but there are things that cannot be changed. One day, I'll tell you how hard it must have been for him, how much he surely misses you…'

Cradling her baby, she stepped into the living area and there was the pink domed palace on the news, and the inevitable view of the goldsmith and mystic stepping out.

She felt sick, watching the ancient ritual, and listened as the excited journalist relayed that gold had successfully been removed from the dome last night, and that before the sun set a second time, a wedding must take place, or Al-Zahan would be no more.

There was even a little countdown clock with twenty hours to go.

And there was not a thing Aubrey could do, other than get on with living and providing for their beautiful son.

And so that night, instead of lying on the bed and crying, as she wanted to, she dressed in a silver sequined leotard, put on her make-up and then kissed Aayiz goodbye, but her baby was fretful.

'He's teething,' Mom said. 'See how he's chewing on his fingers.'

'Should I get him something on the way home?' Aubrey asked.

'I'll go now,' Aunt Carmel said.

Aubrey's baby was looked after by so many, for his great-aunt would take a bus and go to the drug store, rather than have him cry in pain.

'He'll be fine,' Stella reassured her daughter when Aubrey had to head off. 'Don't fret.'

Yet Aayiz was not fine.

He cried and he fretted and his little cheeks turned red as he gnawed on his fingers and he cried into the night. When there was a knock on the door, Stella groaned in relief. 'That will be Aunt Carmel,' she crooned.

Only it wasn't.

It was a man, dark and unshaven and in robes of silver, and Stella knew exactly who this was, for with one look she knew he could only be the father of the baby she held in her arms.

'Get away!' Stella shouted. 'Get back...'

'Ms Johnson,' Khalid implored. 'I am not here

to take him, I am here to see Aubrey.' But first he saw his son.

His little Prince and the rightful heir. His heart cleaved at the sight of him. Stella saw the love in his eyes and after a moment's stand-off invited him in.

Khalid looked at the neat home, with pictures of Aubrey lining the walls, and a couple of Jobe too, and there were some of Aayiz and plenty of Stella before the fire had ravaged her face.

'I came to ask your permission to ask Aubrey to be my wife.'

'Your wife?' Stella checked, and then she swallowed, for she knew now not just that this was her grandson's father but she had worked out just who he was. After all, she had closely watched Jobe's funeral on the news.

'Yes, but first, before you answer me, may I hold my son?'

Aayiz needed his father, for he instantly soothed to his strong embrace, and he looked up with recognition and already adored the man who held him.

His crying hushed and he simply gazed, and Khalid would never again deny him, whatever the cost.

CHAPTER FIFTEEN

'How's Haris?' asked her friends on her return to work.

And Aubrey told them he would now be called Aayiz.

'Are you okay?' they checked.

'Just tired.'

Of course she was tired.

They knew why Aayiz's mother was working deep into the night—after all, many of them were doing the same.

Aubrey chalked her hands and feet and climbed onto the platform. She took to the trapeze and performed her routine the very best that she could, with a heart that at first felt very heavy.

Yet Aubrey actually liked the trapeze.

She shut out the gamblers below and the smoke and the noise, and made plans for her and Aayiz.

Tomorrow she would call Philippe.

She would ask him to consider her for spots abroad now and then, opening shows and expos and things so she would be away for only a few days at a time.

In the interim she could concentrate on her music.

Aubrey tipped backwards and hung by her knees and swung high. The hours were being counted down and as she swung and hung and twisted, she thought of how she'd taunted Khalid about being with someone else.

And now the biter would be bit.

She was certain.

There were no clocks in the casino but to hazard a guess, in sixteen or so hours Khalid would take his chosen bride.

She sat back up on the swing and kicked off again; with increasing momentum she kicked her legs and again tipped back.

And she was most certainly seeing things for now there was a huge man in silver and black robes, and heads were turning, for even in Vegas Khalid stood out.

Now she swung and she taunted, not the gamblers below but the man who approached and then stood beneath her. Aubrey didn't quite know why, but she kicked her legs, and she dazzled.

'Aubrey!' His voice was deep, and still measured. 'May I ask that you get down?'

She ignored him.

Terrified and knowing that if she did then history really would repeat itself, she stayed where she was.

It was safer up here.

And so she kicked her legs harder and then hung by her hands and stretched her legs wide apart.

'Aubrey,' he said, and the gaming table stilled at the authority in his voice. The croupiers at other tables stopped dealing, and her friends started to come over. 'Get down.'

She sat on the swing and looked down, and she defied him. 'No.'

Beside him stood a robed man, and Laisha as well as two bodyguards that Aubrey had seen at Jobe's funeral.

They all looked stressed.

It was clear that none were used to the Sheikh Prince not getting his way.

And neither was Khalid. His patience was starting to wear thin, for he wanted her to hear what he had to say.

He took a step and started to climb onto the platform. It was completely forbidden for him to do so, but the casino's own security were standing back and so was Vince, for it was clear no one could stop Khalid.

'I'm not coming down,' Aubrey said, though she was only swinging gently now. 'Go and choose your wife, Khalid…'

'I have chosen my wife,' Khalid said.

'And I have to live with it?' Aubrey angrily checked. 'Are you hoping for a quickie while you're still single?' From the gasps from his entourage, she should not be speaking that way, and they clearly expected their Prince to deliver a terse warning.

Yet he smiled. 'Aubrey, the bride I have chosen is you.'

She stopped swinging as the enormity of his words hit her, especially when Laisha started crying and imploring Khalid in Arabic, and the men in robes seemed overcome.

'Your father...' Aubrey gulped, and then her eyes pleaded with him as she reminded him of the consequences if she agreed to marry him. 'Hussain...'

'Just tell me that you will be my bride,' Khalid said. 'And I will deal with the King, Aubrey, I will take care of everything and everyone.'

'Even me?'

'Especially you,' Khalid said. 'And my beautiful son Aayiz. If you will allow me to.'

'Yes!'

And when he held out his arms she dropped into them, just fell into his strong embrace and slid down the solid wall of his body till their lips were together again.

The gamblers, the croupiers and especially her friends were all applauding and cheering, but it did not compare to the roar in her ears as he stopped kissing her and lifted her over his shoulder and took her out to the Strip, where a sheikh prince and a trapeze artist barely merited a glance.

'It will be okay,' he told her over and over when she started to cry.

'How can it be?' Aubrey asked, and tears filled her eyes. 'Poor Hussain.'

'No,' Khalid reassured her. 'Hussain will be fine…'

'But Abbad…' Her heart twisted for she too had seen the dart of fear in Abbad's eyes. It was Khalid who had been born to be King, who wanted to be King, and she couldn't bear that their love would cause hurt.

'I have spoken with the King,' Khalid said. He put a hand on a pillar and shielded her petite body from the masses so that it felt as if it was only them. 'He reminded me that if my wedding does not take place by the second sunset, then Al-Zahan will be no more, and I pointed out that the mainland people were happy and were ruled by a wise and kind queen…'

She felt as though Khalid was the biggest gambler in Vegas when he told her what he had done.

'I told the King that if he did not approve you as my bride, then Hussain did not want my role and neither did Abbad. That we would be more than willing to unite with the people of the mainland; that I had spoken with the Queen and would remain an ambassador to my people…'

'No,' Aubrey whispered.

'Aubrey,' Khalid said, 'I pointed out that you have worn my scent for a year, that an amulet was given to us by Jobe on the day our son was conceived. Aayiz is my son and I shall never again deny him.'

'But you want to be King.'

'Only if you are my Queen. If the King does not approve, then the Al-Zahan kingdom ends. Better a kind queen and strong ambassador than a cold and cruel king…'

Aubrey could feel her heart trying to escape her chest as she realised the lengths to which Khalid would go for them to be together.

'No!' she pleaded, scared now of what she had unleashed.

But then Khalid smiled and the world felt right. 'That is exactly what my father said,' Khalid said. 'The bastard was on his knees, imploring me to take you as my wife…' He ached to kiss her but he could not. 'Aubrey, we have to leave now. It shall soon be morning in Al-Zahan…' He turned to his people, but Laisha shook her head.

'There is not enough time, it is eighteen flying hours and we only have fifteen until sunset,' she told him. 'Al-Zahan will fall…'

The aide started frantically rushing them to a car,

'If we leave now,' Khalid said, 'we could still make it. I shall speak to the pilot—'

But Aubrey had a better idea.

'Khalid.' She interrupted the secretary and the aides and even the future King. She stood in her sparkly leotard in the middle of the Strip and reminded them all of a gorgeous fact. 'We're in Vegas.'

'The people must witness your union,' Laisha said.

'And they shall.' Khalid smiled.

He kissed Aubrey's face, he kissed her eyes, he held her sequined hips in his strong hands and kissed her mouth. He released her, but Aubrey's hands were knotted behind his neck.

'Let go,' he said.

'Never.'

'I mean it, Aubrey.' Khalid prised off her hands and sobered her, drunk with love and lust, with his words. 'There is a *royal* wedding to be arranged.'

It was daunting and terrifying but then he whispered in her ear.

'And then I'll make love to you.'

CHAPTER SIXTEEN

A ROYAL WEDDING in fifteen hours!

It might seem impossible but Aubrey was part of a sisterhood, and they all pulled together for this most spectacular event.

Brandy made several calls, and the lavish venue was chosen.

Khalid liaised with the elders, who were surprisingly thrilled with the refreshing change, for they had seen the cruel ways of the King and had silently dreaded that their Sheikh Prince might one day turn his back on the land they all loved.

But all that took time.

With a baby to feed and a father who wanted to do it for the first time.

Aubrey watched as Khalid sat on the sofa in their tiny home and gave a hungry Aayiz his bottle.

'He's tiny,' Khalid said.

He certainly looked it in his father's arms.

'I hate it that you went through all of this alone.'

There wasn't time, there just wasn't, but Aubrey

went and sat on Khalid's knee and looked down at their son being held by his father.

'I love being his mom,' Aubrey said, and then she realised she hadn't yet told Khalid just how deeply she felt. 'I love you, Khalid, so very much.'

They were the words he needed to hear, and he wanted her so much—and to give those words their due—but with six hours to go it was time to separate.

'I can do my own make-up,' Aubrey said, ticking things off, 'but I want Mom's hair done and...' She panicked. 'I have to find a dress.'

'You go and sort out your dress and your wedding party,' Khalid told her. 'I will take care of the rest.'

'What about flowers?'

'Go!' Khalid said.

'Should you really leave it all to him?' Stella checked, though loud enough for Khalid to hear.

'Stella,' Khalid said in his rich deep voice to his future mother-in-law, 'I will take care of everything.'

The smile he gave told Stella that she did not have to worry now.

Khalid was left delightedly holding his baby as the women headed off with a diamond clip full of his cash to get ready for the wedding.

Aubrey chose a dress in the purest white that swept the floor, even in heels.

'You look beautiful.' her mom said with tears in her eyes. 'Aubrey, I am so happy for you. You deserve this.'

'So did you, Mom,' Aubrey said, and they hugged and Aubrey understood her mom so much better now.

For the first time since the accident, her mom's hair was skilfully styled, and a small hairpiece, carefully blended, made such a difference and covered some of the most loathed scars. Then the colour technician performed his own brand of magic on Aunt Carmel's red and white hair.

And then it was Aubrey's turn and she chose to wear it up, so it showed her silver locket to best effect, though a few subtle curls were let loose.

With less than an hour to go, there was a knock on the door to their sumptuous hotel suite and Aubrey found herself smiling at Vanda, the make-up artist who had helped Aubrey that day in New York.

'By royal appointment,' Vanda squealed, and did a happy dance in the corridor outside.

Brandy had said she would organise the flowers, but when a bouquet of peonies arrived in soft whites and the palest blush pinks, Aubrey knew that Khalid had chosen them, for they were the same type of flowers that had been on the table at their New York City dinner on the night they had met and made love.

'You're going to take his breath away,' Vanda said as they made their way down.

Vegas had everything, and that included luxury.

Stella worked here every day, and Aubrey had been here on occasion, but she had never thought she might marry here.

Had never thought that she would be surrounded

by family and friends and that her gorgeous Prince would stand waiting for her, holding their son.

Khalid wore an embellished robe of rose-gold and a *kefeyah* and to Aubrey he seemed more beautiful each and every day. Aayiz wore deep navy and they looked so handsome and so full of love that Aubrey had to rely on her mom's hand on her arm not to run to them.

'Slowly,' Stella reminded her. 'Enjoy your moment, Aubrey.'

Aubrey was so proud of her mom, who had dreamt of this day for herself but was so thrilled to be here instead for her daughter.

She saw his brothers and sister there, and they smiled so widely as she walked on her mom's arm to the gorgeous strains of Brandy and her wonderful girlfriends singing 'The Wonder of You'.

Oh, it made her cry. It was the perfect song, especially when sung by dear friends, and as she reached Khalid's side, she touched his hand, the man who would one day be King.

'Did you choose this?' Aubrey asked Khalid.

'I accepted Brandy's suggestion.'

She was glad that he had.

And then a huge screen lit up and she realised just how busy Khalid and his aides had been, for there was a live stream from the palace. They stood as if beside the golden dome, and heard the cheers of the crowd as their Prince and his chosen bride first came into view.

It was a wedding Khalid had never envisaged, yet it made complete and perfect sense, for he loved her, every facet of her, and when the elders spoke to gathered family and friends, Laisha translated the words whispered over centuries in the Al-Zahan desert.

All his life, Khalid had wanted for nothing.

Save love.

All her life, Aubrey had wanted for everything.

Save love.

Khalid dressed her finger and wrist in a hand flower bracelet made of gold from the palace.

When Khalid spoke, his words were measured and clear.

'Aubrey, I shall provide for you, and I shall care for you.' Then he told her more than Al-Zahan law required him to. 'I offer you my love.'

A critic might say he was a touch emotionless in his delivery.

But that critic did not know Khalid.

'Khalid, I accept your love,' Aubrey said, and she looked down at their entwined hands, and she had to actually remind herself to breathe, for the air seemed trapped in her throat.

They were officially married now.

It was still morning in Vegas when they left their reception.

But the hour didn't matter.

It was night time in Al-Zahan and there were celebrations there too, for not only was their beloved Crown Prince now married, there was a new prince too.

Prince Aayiz.

He lay now, in another luxury suite, being watched over by his devoted nanny and aunt.

And finally it was just them.

He undressed her slowly.

The gorgeous white dress dropped to the floor, and she felt too short when she took off her heels and faced Khalid and watched as he removed his fine robes.

And when he was naked she told him something. 'I nearly said yes to being your *ikbal.*'

She blushed in shame at her own weakness and then she put her jewelled hand up to his chest and he pulled her in and kissed her trembling mouth.

He kissed her onto the vast bed and she sank, and never wanted to come up for air.

He kissed her neck and then the locket, he kissed her breasts and her stomach, made taut from the fingers he slipped inside her.

'Are you telling me you nearly said yes to being my mistress?'

'Yes…' she gasped.

'You nearly said yes?' Khalid checked, removing his skilled fingers and leaning over her, pressing her into the bed with his delicious weight as he spread her legs. 'Yes to living in the desert and being made love to day and night unsheathed?'

'Yes,' Aubrey said as he took her, and she wondered, truly, how she'd ever said no.

'You will always be my favourite and chosen one.'

But then, as she came, she knew.

'I'm your only one, Khalid.'

And she was.

Absolutely, Aubrey knew that she was.

EPILOGUE

'DO YOU MISS HIM?' Aubrey asked.

She often wondered, and sometimes asked, but Khalid always chose not to answer.

But on a day such as today, with the sun high in a blue Al-Zahan sky, with the pomp of the coronation behind them and the most stunning view from the hundredth floor, she wondered if Khalid missed his father, who had passed away.

The hundredth floor!

Aubrey looked as Khalid held not just their tiny new daughter but a fifteen-month-old Aayiz, who frankly, since his sister had been born, to Aubrey looked enormous.

Khalid held them both with ease.

He did not immediately answer.

He looked out to the ocean and the impressive yachts, and to a country where not just the rulers prospered but the people were starting to as well.

There was no bridge to the mainland, of course not, that would be years in the making.

But the surveyors were out.

And today the Queen and her Prince Consort would visit discreetly, for they adored Aubrey. A personal visit. The official one would take place at a later date.

Khalid had never for a second gambled with his people, for he had known the Queen would be a better bet than a prince who had no choice but to wait before he took over from a bitter, toxic king.

He felt Aayiz's hand on his face, and wondered how a father could not turn and smile at that innocent touch.

Then he looked down at his newborn daughter, just four hours old, with impossibly long fingers and a very squashed nose, made up for by her rosebud mouth.

And he loved her from the depths of his soul.

How, Khalid pondered, could a king not want the best for *all* the people he loved?

It hadn't all been plain sailing. Khalid privately struggled with Stella.

The more he heard, the more he had to fight for his neck not to arch.

Yet he fought to see the best in the mother of the woman he loved.

Now Stella lived in a stunning apartment overlooking the Strip and reminisced with Carmel about days of old, and he had ensured the best surgeons had taken care of her scars.

At first he had done that for Aubrey.

Now he did it because…

He cared.

Khalid even smiled when Stella came in without knocking. She had been here for two weeks, awaiting the birth of her second grandchild.

Two weeks, three days, and fifteen hours. God help Khalid.

'I thought I might take Haris to look at the boats,' she said.

It was so much more than his father would have done.

'Aayiz,' Aubrey corrected, for what felt like the millionth time.

'He would love that, Stella,' Khalid said, and handed his son to her. He watched as Stella pulled a funny face and made a serious Aayiz laugh, and then she peered at the new, very tiny baby.

'She looks just like Aubrey when she was first born,' Stella said. 'Well, a bit darker, but she had that nose for a few days.'

Khalid smiled.

His first *real* one for Stella.

The saying fake it till you make it came to mind.

It had worked, for he was starting to like her.

In truth, he admired Stella, for Khalid admired strength and the Johnsons had it in spades.

'Stella,' Khalid said, 'have you spoken to Carmel about coming over now the baby is here?'

'Didn't I tell you?' Stella beamed. 'She's on her way.'

Aubrey would never know why her serious husband suddenly laughed.

She kissed Aayiz, and then Aayiz kissed his new sister.

And Khalid watched as the pantomime of love continued and Stella kissed her daughter then left.

'No,' he said as the door closed.

Aubrey frowned and then pulled her mind back to the conversation they'd been having.

'I don't miss him.'

He came and sat on the bed. She moved her legs to make room and looked at her mysterious man who sometimes didn't give the answer she was looking for.

But then neither did she.

They challenged each other, while adoring each other, and then there were times like these.

Where they both smiled in awe at the life they had made and she wanted to thump his strong arm at how clever they were. 'She's so beautiful. When Aayiz was born…' She stopped.

'Tell me.'

'They whisked him away,' Aubrey said. 'I thought I might never see him again.'

'Look at him now,' Khalid said, and he kissed her tired face. 'Look at the beautiful boy you grew.'

He knew her.

She was a little scared to love and so he handed her their little girl whom he had held for more than four hours now.

'She's not going to disappear.'

Aubrey held her baby properly.

Her tiny girl.

'We have to think of a name,' Khalid prompted.

'She already has one,' Aubrey said. 'Dalila.'

Khalid stilled for a moment, but then he spoke, and when he did Aubrey rested back on her pillows and smiled.

'Abnataya alhabiba,' he whispered to his sleeping baby. 'Beloved daughter, I pray that you will walk in the sun and laugh as I did…'

She would.

* * * * *

If you enjoyed
Claimed for the Sheikh's Shock Son
by Carol Marinelli
you're sure to enjoy these other
Secret Heirs of Billionaires stories!

The Secret Kept from the Italian
by Kate Hewitt
Demanding His Secret Son
by Louise Fuller
The Sheikh's Secret Baby
by Sharon Kendrick
The Sicilian's Secret Son
by Angela Bissell

Available now!

#3721 THE SHEIKH CROWNS HIS VIRGIN
Billionaires at the Altar
by Lynne Graham
When Zoe is kidnapped, she's saved by Raj—an exiled desert prince. The attraction between them is instant! Yet her rescue comes with a price: to avoid a scandal, Zoe *must* become Raj's virgin bride...

#3722 SHOCK HEIR FOR THE KING
Secret Heirs of Billionaires
by Clare Connelly
Frankie is shocked when Matt, the stranger she gave her innocence to, reappears. Now she's in for the biggest shock of all—he's actually *King* Matthias! And to claim his heir, he demands Frankie become his queen!

#3723 GREEK'S BABY OF REDEMPTION
One Night With Consequences
by Kate Hewitt
When brooding billionaire Alex needs a wife to secure his business, his housekeeper, Milly, agrees. But their wedding night sparks an unexpected fire... Could Milly—and his unborn child—be the key to Alex's redemption?

#3724 UNTOUCHED UNTIL HER ULTRA-RICH HUSBAND
by Dani Collins
To avoid destitution, Luli needs outrageously wealthy Gabriel's help. The multi-billionaire's solution? He'll secure both their futures by marrying her! But after sweeping Luli into his luxurious world, Gabriel discovers the chemistry with his untouched wife is *priceless*...

HPCNM0519RA

#3725 A SCANDALOUS MIDNIGHT IN MADRID
Passion in Paradise
by Susan Stephens
A moonlit encounter tempts Sadie all the way to Alejandro's castle...and into his bed! But their night of illicit pleasure soon turns Sadie into Spain's most scandalous headline: *Pregnant with Alejandro's baby!*

#3726 UNTAMED BILLIONAIRE'S INNOCENT BRIDE
Conveniently Wed!
by Caitlin Crews
To prevent a scandal, Lauren needs to find reclusive Dominik—her boss's estranged brother—and convince him to marry her! As Dominik awakens her long-dormant desire, will Lauren accept that their hunger can't be denied?

#3727 CLAIMING HIS REPLACEMENT QUEEN
Monteverre Marriages
by Amanda Cinelli
Khalil's motivation for marriage is politics, not passion. Yet a sizzling encounter with his soon-to-be queen, Cressida, changes everything. And the desire innocent Cressida ignites is too hot to resist...

#3728 REUNITED BY THE GREEK'S VOWS
by Andie Brock
Kate is stunned when ex-fiancé, Nikos, storms back into her life—and demands they marry! Desperate to save her company, she agrees. But what these heated adversaries don't anticipate is that their still-smoldering flame will explode into irresistible passion...

YOU CAN FIND MORE INFORMATION ON UPCOMING HARLEQUIN® TITLES, FREE EXCERPTS AND MORE AT WWW.HARLEQUIN.COM.

HPCNM0519RB

You told me what you were worth, Luli. Act like you believe it.

She had been acting. The whole time. Still was, especially as a handful
of designers whose names she knew from Mae's glossy magazines behaved
with deference as they welcomed her to a private showroom complete with
catwalk.

She had to fight back laughing with incredulity as they offered her
champagne, caviar, even a pedicure.

"I—" She glanced at Gabriel, expecting him to tell them she aspired to
model and should be treated like a clotheshorse, not royalty.

"A full wardrobe," he said. "Top to bottom, morning to night, office to
evening. Do what you can overnight, then send the rest to my address in
New York."

"Mais bien sûr, monsieur," the couturier said without a hint of falter in
her smile. "Our pleasure."

"Gabriel—" Luli started to protest as the women scattered.

"You remember what I said about this?" He tapped the wallet that held
her phone. "I need you to stay on brand."

"Reflect who you are?"

"Yes."

"Who are you?" she asked ruefully. "I only met you ten minutes ago."

"I'm a man who doesn't settle for anything less than the best." He
touched her chin. "The world is going to have a lot of questions about why
we married. Give them an answer."

His words roused the competitor who still lurked inside her. She wanted to prove to the world she was worthy to be his wife. Maybe she wanted to prove her worth to him, too. Definitely she longed to prove something to herself.

Either way, she made sure those long-ago years of preparation paid off. She had always been ruthless in evaluating her own shortcomings and knew how to play to her strengths. She might not be trying to win a crown today, but she hadn't been then, either. She'd been trying to win the approval of a woman who hadn't deserved her idolatry.

She pushed aside those dark memories and clung instead to the education she had gained in those difficult years.

"That neckline will make my shoulders look narrow," she said, making quick up-and-down choices. "The sweetheart style is better, but no ruffles at my hips. Don't show me yellow. Tangerine is better. A more verdant green. That one is too pale." In her head, she was sectioning out the building blocks of a cohesive stage presence. Youthful, but not too trendy. Sensual, but not overtly sexual. Charismatic without being showy.

"Something tells me I'm not needed," Gabriel said twenty minutes in and rose to leave. "We'll go for dinner in three hours." He glanced to the couturier. "And return in the morning for another fitting."

"Parfait. Merci, monsieur." Her smile was calm, but the way people were bustling told Luli how big a deal this was. How big a deal Gabriel was.

The women took her measurements while showing her unfinished pieces that only needed hemming or minimal tailoring so she could take them immediately.

"You'll be up all night," Luli murmured to one of the seamstresses.

The young woman moved quickly, but not fast enough for her boss, who kept crying, *"Vite! Vite!"*

"I'm sorry to put you through this," Luli added.

"Pas de problème. Monsieur Dean is a treasured client. It's our honor to provide your trousseau." She clamped her teeth on a pin between words. "Do you know where he's taking you for dinner? We should choose that dress next, so I can work on the alterations while you have your hair and makeup done. It must be fabulous. The world will be watching."

She would be presented publicly as his wife, Luli realized with a hard thump in her heart.

Don't miss
Untouched Until Her Ultra-Rich Husband.
Available June 2019 wherever
Harlequin® Presents books and ebooks are sold.

www.Harlequin.com

HPEXP0519

HARLEQUIN

Presents.®

Coming next month—
a seductive Spanish romance!

In *A Scandalous Midnight in Madrid* by Susan Stephens,
Sadie is shocked by the red-hot connection she feels when
she encounters the aristocratic Spanish billionaire.
But what's even more shocking, is when she discovers
that she's pregnant with his baby...

Dedicated chef Sadie's life is changed forever by an
intense moonlit encounter in Madrid with infamous
Alejandro de Alegon. The sizzling anticipation he sparks
tempts virgin Sadie all the way to his Spanish castle...and
into his bed! She's never known anything like the wild passion
Alejandro unleashes. But when Sadie discovers their night of
illicit pleasure had consequences, she becomes Spain's biggest
headline: scandalously pregnant with Alejandro's baby!

A Scandalous Midnight in Madrid

Passion in Paradise

Available June 2019

HPBPA0519